This story really happened.

On June 28, 1940, the Norwegian freighter *Bomma* reached Baltimore with a cargo of gold bullion worth $9,000,000.

When the *Bomma*'s captain asked for a police escort while unloading the bullion, a strange story came to light. The gold, it was learned, had been slipped past Nazi sentries by Norwegian boys and girls! Under the very eyes of the enemy, these children had pulled the gold on their sleds to a freighter hidden in a fiord off Norway's coast. That no harm might come to the brave children, the captain did not tell the location of the fiord.

Some names and details have been changed, but this is a true story. It is a stirring tale of courage shown by real children who helped their country in a time of great danger.

To a skilled craftsman and understanding friend

RUTH AYERS ROUNDS

and to her HAROLD and EMILY

SNOW

TREASURE

(The Rescue of the Hidden Gold)

By MARIE McSWIGAN

Illustrated by André LaBlanc

SCHOLASTIC BOOK SERVICES

NEW YORK · TORONTO · LONDON · AUCKLAND · SYDNEY · TOKYO

Other books by Marie McSwigan

Hi, Barney!

All Aboard for Freedom!

Three's a Crowd*

* *Available from Scholastic Book Services*

ISBN: 0-590-03132-5

Copyright 1942 by E. P. Dutton & Co., Inc. Copyright © 1958 by TAB Books, Inc. This edition is published by Scholastic Book Services, a division of Scholastic Magazines, Inc., by arrangement with E. P. Dutton & Co., Inc.

29 28 27 26   3 4 5/8
                                                                         01

Printed in the U.S.A.

CHAPTER ONE

"**B**EAT you to the turn!" Peter Lundstrom shot his sled down the long steep slope.

"No fair. You started first," his friend, Michael Berg, protested. Nevertheless, he flew along in Peter's tracks.

School was over for that day at least, and Peter and Michael were enjoying one of the sled rides the children of Norway never seem to tire of.

At the turn they paused for breath. But their rest was short for Peter spied another sled.

"Look out! Here come the girls!" With that he headed down another slope, his friend behind him.

Peter was twelve and felt grown up. Playing with girls was something he meant never to do. Heavy clothes hid all but his yellow hair and his face. His eyes were clear and brown. Wide apart and in an even line, they looked untroubled.

Michael, the same age, seemed different in everything else. While Peter was tall and slender, Michael was square. His hair was like tow and his eyes were that bright blue that is often called "typically Scandinavian."

"Hey—wait a minute!" A dark-eyed girl drove her sled into the place the boys had just left. Her black curls bobbed like sausages under the cherry red of her hood. She was Helga Thomsen and somewhat of a tomboy. Behind her on the same sled was a smaller girl, fair as

Helga was dark. The smaller girl was Lovisa, Peter's ten-year-old sister.

"We'll catch them at the lookout. Hold on!" Helga dug her heels into the snow and began another swift descent.

Catch them at the lookout they did, for the sled track made a sharp twist; and below that, nearly a thousand feet, lay the sea. Peter and Michael had to slow down to avoid crashing a wall that protected the road.

Helga, daring as any boy, drove straight at them so there was a clamor of yells and a tangle of windbreakers, caps, sweaters and mittens.

There never had been such a winter for snow!

It began early and with each month grew higher and higher on the ground. April was like January, with no sign of thaw. From one end of Norway to the other, people talked of nothing else. They only stopped talking about it when something entirely terrifying drove it from their minds. Then they remembered it again and looked to it to help them in their trouble.

Up in the Arctic Circle where these children lived, it was winter for much of the year. Sleds and skis were used for travel for all but a few months. But accustomed as the people were to the long cold and the white stillness, the winter of 1940 surpassed anything even the oldest could remember.

The mountains seemed asleep that April. Along the sea the world was lifeless. Except for the fiords, the harbors here in the north were ice-locked, their channels great fields of white. The fiords alone seemed alive with their black rushing waters and bobbing ice cakes. These

2

forceful streams flow too fast for freezing and so are always a highway to the open sea.

The four friends at the lookout continued their lively play. Peter and Michael tried to wash Helga's face but the snow was too hard and dry and the face washing could hardly have been called successful. Helga managed to get a handful of snow down Peter's back and that *did* amount to something, for he had a bit of trouble shaking it out to prevent the discomfort of its melting.

Tired of the tussle, the four squatted on their sleds. When Michael idly tossed a lump of snow in Helga's lap she got up to shake her dress. In doing so she turned toward the sea.

"Why, Peter, there's your Uncle Victor!" She was surprised. "And Rolls, his mate! Look!"

"You're crazy!" Peter didn't bother to get up.

"But it *is* your Uncle Victor. Honest!"

"Now what in the world would he be doing here? You don't suppose he's fishing this time of the year, do you?"

"But it is, Peter. Come, see."

She was so sure about it that he got up, if only to be able to tell her she was wrong.

Below, miles away by road but only a little distance for a stone, Uncle Victor was making footprints in the hard snow. Behind him was the stocky figure of Rolls, second in command of the Lundstrom fishing fleet.

"Yoo hoo, Uncle Victor!" Lovisa was on her feet and looking out over the wall of the lookout. But she could not make him hear.

"Yoo hoo," the four of them yelled in chorus, cupping their hands to make the sound carry farther.

Then Victor Lundstrom heard them and looked up. But there was no great roar of greeting the children had expected. He only waved his arm and went on walking. Rolls saw them, too, and gave an equally casual salute.

Peter scowled. The greeting was unlike Uncle Victor. Why he should have been overjoyed to see them, especially after a long trip! He was Peter's favorite relative and, in all truth, his hero. He led a life of adventure in contrast with Peter's father, a banker. He was one of the most successful fishermen in that land of able fishers. He had a whole fleet of boats and sailed about everywhere, his nephew supposed. When he came back from a voyage he had stories to tell that no one could match. Uncle Victor was as fond of his brother's children as they were of him. So it wasn't like him not to seem glad to see them.

"What's he doing here?" Michael wanted to know.

They watched him walk along the beach toward the cliff beyond Riswyk Fiord.

"He's on his way to the Snake," they decided.

The Snake was a tiny arm of the big fiord so twisted and narrow that it deserved its name. Unless you knew about the Snake you never would have guessed it was there. Almost entirely hidden by cliffs, even from the air it would be hard to trace.

"To the *Cleng Peerson*," Lovisa's eyes danced, for the *Cleng Peerson* was Uncle Victor's own fishing boat, the one that he alone might sail. The children were permitted aboard only as a special treat.

"But why is he here?" Peter pondered. "He never

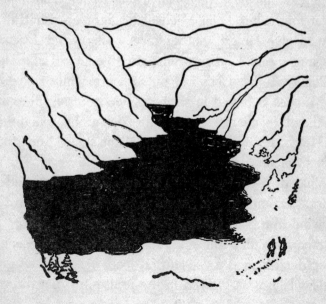

comes north until the ice is gone." But he had no time for further reflection when a snowball broke in his face.

"So you thought I was crazy!" Helga taunted.

"Crazy as a hare!" Michael's snowball landed on Helga's hood. It spattered and her eyes and face were white. She lowered her head and shook it from side to side like a fierce young animal and then she charged at her tormentor.

Meanwhile Lovisa had not been idle. Her fast moving mittens were busy rolling hard pellets of snow. Then she stood back and hurled with all her strength and all the skill she had been able to acquire by watching and imitating the boys since she was old enough to remember.

Helga and Peter were locked in a tussle when Lovisa came to her friend's rescue. One swift ball caught Peter on the ear and he turned, surprised, to see who his assailant might be. Then Michael brought up a hatful of snow to give Helga another face washing but Lovisa's ball caught him so abruptly he stumbled and fell.

"Come, Helga. Let's get out of here while we're on top." Lovisa believed in securing her victories. She preferred not to chance a smashing defeat by remaining. But Helga parted her feet in a defiant stance and stood ready to meet all comers.

"What do you want to run away for?" she jeered at Lovisa. "I should think anyone who could hit as hard as you would be glad to stay and fight it out."

Here was high tribute. It came from one who was not only older but was a recognized leader among the girls of Riswyk. Lovisa glowed in the praise but that did not

6

stop her busy mittens. They were piling many rounds of ammunition on Helga's sled.

"Look out!" Helga warned just in time to prevent Peter stealing the sled and all the snowballs. So Peter got the first of Lovisa's "bullets" and had to stand cross fire when Helga opened from the other side.

And so, the battle went on. The boys, for all their strength and size, did not seem able to subdue the quick-witted girls, and none of them seemed to tire of the brisk exchange of snow.

"Good glory, it's getting dark!" Peter was first to realize that the afternoon was over. Absorbed in the fight, the four of them failed to note the passing time. "We're all going to be late for supper and we'll get what's coming to us." What that was, he didn't have to explain for they all understood it was no pleasant prospect. "Come on. Let's get out of here."

There was a scramble for sleds, caps, mittens and even sweaters that had been discarded as the battle grew hot. Then began the long climb up the mountain to Riswyk, the town that stood on a level shelf on the mountain slope.

As Peter predicted, he and Lovisa were late for their evening meal. But "what's coming to us" never came. Their father was busy with his own thoughts and their mother could always be counted on to keep peace in the family, especially when Mr. Lundstrom was home.

When they told of seeing Uncle Victor, a strange thing happened.

Their father pushed back his chair and jumped up from the table. Peter and Lovisa were surprised because they had never before seen him leave a meal unfinished.

"My hat and coat, Per Garson," he called to the old family servant. "Victor's back from Oslo. I've got to go out!"

Per Garson, entering with the coffee, all but dropped the tray.

CHAPTER TWO

WHEN Peter told his father about seeing Uncle Victor that afternoon he saw a look of alarm come over his face.

Now that was strange because, although the two brothers were different in every way, there was a strong bond between them.

Was Uncle Victor in some sort of trouble? Peter wondered. But when he asked his mother she shook her head.

"Well, why did Father go out?" he asked. "You know he never does at night. He says he's tired after a day at the bank and likes to stay home."

"Yes, I know," his mother replied, "and he's busier than ever right now and so must be very tired. A treasury official has been here from Oslo and your father has had to work very hard. He's worried."

"Is it because we're going to be poor?" Lovisa asked. "Is there something wrong with the bank?" For Lovisa and Peter had always lived in horror of "something wrong with the bank."

"Not that I know of, Lovisa," her mother answered. "The bank has more gold than ever."

"Well, then why is Father worried? He used to play a lot with Bunny." Peter referred to his four-year-old brother. "Now he hardly even notices him. Is it about the war?" he asked as an afterthought. "About the Nazis taking Poland?" For even up in the Arctic Circle the disturbance of that year could not be overlooked.

"Yes, Peter. It has something to do with that. But don't worry. Your father's a capable man. Everything he gets his hands on turns out all right."

Peter was awakened out of a sound sleep that night. To his room came the tramp of heavy boots. Then bang, bang, bang, bang, boots kicked the outside wall to shake off snow. Then there was more banging of the storm doors and the house door as well. Then came voices.

He wondered what could be the matter. He got up to see. It was unlike anything he could remember to have people coming into the house late at night.

His father was speaking when Peter got to the door of the living room. He was bent over the hearth raking the embers of the dying fire. Per Garson, the old house man, shuffled in and took the fire irons away from him.

"They'll never get our gold!" His father turned to face the men he had brought home with him. His voice was low and hoarse. "Not an ounce of it will they touch! Of that I am determined."

"How much does it amount to, now that the last shipment is here?" John Olsen, the clock maker, asked.

"It's bullion, of course," Mr. Lundstrom replied, "and it's more than thirteen tons." And Peter was banker's son enough to know that bullion is the gold before it is made into money.

"Thirteen tons!" Michael Berg's father exclaimed. "Why that would be thirty million kroner!"

"More," his father replied. "It's nearer forty millions."

"Whew!" came a whistle and Peter saw his Uncle

Victor. "That's around nine million dollars in the United States." Uncle Victor had spent much time in America. He and Peter's father had a brother in Minnesota, and Victor had visited there. More often than not he spoke of dollars, rather than of the Norwegian coin, the krone.

Peter made a move into the room and it was then they saw him.

"Peter," his father spoke harshly. "Go back to bed. And close the door."

"Wait a minute, Lars," Uncle Victor addressed his older brother. "Peter's nearly thirteen. It's Peter and the ones his age who can save our gold. I see it now. Why didn't we think of it before? We've spent the night considering everything from reindeer sleds to tri-motor planes. And here we have the answer right under our noses—the children."

They looked at Uncle Victor in surprise. But he only stepped up and put his arm around Peter's shoulders.

"This is no boys' game," his father spoke less sharply and when he looked at Peter there was sadness in his eyes. "Go to bed, son." His voice was kind.

"Wait, Lars. Let me talk to Peter. When he goes to bed I'll show you how we're going to save our bullion." He drew Peter toward the fire and threw a coat over his pajamas.

"How many children in Riswyk School, Peter? Forty?"

"There're nearer fifty, Uncle Victor."

"How many do you suppose are over ten?"

"Oh, gee whiz, Uncle Victor, I don't know. Maybe half. You mean girls, too?"

"Of course I mean girls, too." He spoke hurriedly. "Now, Peter, when I was a boy we thought nothing of a sled trip to the Snake. It's nine miles but we were young and tough. Not soft like you. We thought nothing of a trip like that."

"We go to the Snake, too," Peter retorted, glaring. He never knew when Uncle Victor was teasing him.

"Of course you wouldn't start at Riswyk. There'd be two or three miles before you started. That makes, maybe twelve miles. Think you could do it or would you be crying for Mama all the time?"

"Uncle Victor, I don't know what you're talking about. But I know that Michael and I and lots of others have been on sled trips that lasted a week. And we didn't cry for our mamas, either."

"You'll do, boy. You're all right. But there's another part, and that's the dangerous part."

"Victor, for all the gold in Norway I won't have my son in danger," Mr. Lundstrom cut in.

"Peter wants a chance to help his country, too. Don't you, fellow?"

Peter nodded. He wouldn't trust his voice.

"So you wouldn't mind if you met an enemy—one that carried a gun?"

Peter was breathless. His eyes were bright. This was the way Uncle Victor lived! There was excitement wherever he was!

"And you wouldn't tell, would you, Peter? They could pull your tongue out and you'd never say a word that would hurt your country?"

"Victor!" Mr. Lundstrom protested. "Enough of this! I know what you mean and it may be our only chance. But don't go on frightening Peter."

"You're all right, youngster, you'll do!" Uncle Victor gave Peter a terrible thump on the back.

CHAPTER THREE

W HEN Peter went back to bed he was far too excited to sleep.

What was Uncle Victor planning?

It was some dangerous scheme, whatever it was; and somehow, he, Peter, was in it, too.

It was a way to save thirteen tons of gold bullion for Norway. That was all he could understand. But how he was going to do it was more than he could hope to know.

The men's voices were low. He could hear only a buzz. He lay thinking of Uncle Victor's words.

It was about going to the Snake on a sled, he remembered. The Snake was where Uncle Victor kept his boat, so perhaps he wanted to put the gold on the boat and sail away. But in that case, why didn't he do it himself? What did he want of Peter?

Uncle Victor could sail away, all right, for the fiords were open all winter and he was the best navigator in the world. It must be that he wanted Peter to carry the thirteen tons of gold on his sled to the boat. But if he took as much as he could on every trip he supposed he'd be an old man before he was finished.

"Say!" he sat up in bed. "He asked how many children in Riswyk School. So that's what he means! All are to help! Even the girls!"

Peter fell asleep figuring how long it would take twenty-five boys and girls to carry thirteen tons of gold

—for how long a distance did Uncle Victor say? For twelve miles. It was a strange problem, for he had no idea how much they could carry at a time. Some of the boys had awfully rickety sleds that wouldn't hold much more than themselves. He guessed he probably could carry seventy-five pounds. But little fellows like Ole Svensen and Nils Larsen couldn't take half that, even downhill.

"Lucky it's downhill and not up," was Peter's last thought before he was sledding down a mountain of dreams.

The next day he tried to find out what had brought Uncle Victor back from Olso so suddenly. But neither his father nor his mother would tell. They were talking in low voices when he got to the breakfast table.

"But not Lovisa," his mother was saying. "I couldn't bear to have Lovisa out of my sight."

"Yes, and Lovisa," his father was saying. "We talked all through the night. Victor's right. For days I've been trying to figure a way out, and Victor hit it his first night home. It's the only way if we're caught—if something happens before we're ready."

"Why did Uncle Victor come back from Oslo?" Peter asked.

"He always comes back in April," his father answered.

"Not when there's this much ice."

"Well, ask him." His father drank his coffee and rose from the table.

On the way to school Peter and Lovisa saw an unusual sight in the town square. Uncle Victor and a crowd of men were building a wooden shed right beside the statue of King Haakon.

"And another one on the north and one on the far side and a big one near the school for the children." Uncle Victor was talking to the postman.

"Why hello, Uncle Victor." Lovisa had not seen her uncle as Peter had, the night before. "What are you doing?"

"Air-raid shelters," he explained.

"Is that why you've come back from Oslo?"

"Partly. They've built a lot of these in the south."

"Are the Germans coming, Uncle Victor? Or would it be the Russians, like in Finland?"

"Hardly either, Lovisa. Certainly not the Germans. Way up here in the Arctic Circle's too far even for them."

"Then it must be the Russians."

"No, Lovisa. It's not the Russians."

"Then why are you building air-raid shelters if it's not the Russians and it's too far for the Germans?"

Uncle Victor had to smile at what he called the relentless logic of childhood. "It's always well to be prepared," he answered. "If you're prepared it won't matter if they do come."

"But it's silly if they're too far away."

At school that day, it was hard to put one's mind on lessons. All the children knew of the air-raid shelters and wanted to talk of nothing else. There was a feeling of restlessness that no one could explain away. Some of the primer class were in tears and had to be sent home, and often an older brother or sister had to go along.

Mr. Anders, the schoolmaster, tried to comfort his pupils. He said that air-raid shelters were found in every country, but here they were only a precaution. He was sure they would never be used.

"Norway's safe from war," he said. "Our country's been at peace for over a hundred years. We've no quarrel with anyone and no one has a quarrel with us. Let's not worry about a thing as unlikely as war."

There was a knock on the classroom door. Uncle Victor came in. He was a great favorite with all the children. When he visited the school he always told a sea story, and so today they settled back for one of his salty tales. But it was no sea story that brought Captain Lundstrom on this occasion. He whispered a few words to Mr. Anders and then spoke to the class.

"Now that we're building bomb shelters, we ought to have an air-raid drill," he said. "We want to teach everyone to go in orderly fashion to the shelters and not be crowding the doorways."

"Just like a fire drill," Mr. Anders said.

"Just like a fire drill," Uncle Victor repeated. "In a fire drill you have your leaders and lieutenants. So with an air-raid drill. Now besides the boys and girls of this school learning to take care of themselves and not be a worry to their parents, there are other things they can do for their country. For that reason I'm going to help you form a club."

If he had promised to sail his boat to the moon he could not have had a quieter audience.

"You want to know what kind of club? Well, for lack of a better name we'll call it the Defense Club. Your president you must obey in everything. You must do all he asks and must never question him. For your president I am going to appoint Peter Lundstrom."

CHAPTER FOUR

"GET UP, Peter. Put your clothes on." His father was shaking him.

The lights were lit. The clock on the mantle showed it was after midnight.

"Dress warmly, too. We're going out."

"Out? Out where?" Peter found it hard to understand why he would be going out after midnight.

"Come on. Dress quickly. I'll tell you as we go."

"Have the Germans come then?" he asked.

"No, of course not. It was only that idea of Uncle Victor's."

"Oh, you mean the Defense Club?" Peter guessed.

"Defense Club?" his father seemed to have forgotten about that although Peter had told him that very afternoon.

"Yes, we formed the Defense Club. Every boy and girl in school is supposed to take orders from me. I'm the president."

"Peter, will you hurry? We've no time to talk about things like that. I've come a long distance to get you because we've just had word that the time is getting very short."

Peter remembered that his father had gone out after supper that night as he had one other night, in haste and clearly troubled. Now he had come back for him, Peter.

They strapped on their skis at the door in the light from the house.

"Aren't you going to take your flashlight, Father?"

"I have it here. But I won't use it unless I have to."

"Spies, Father?"

"We can't be too careful. The success of what we're doing depends on secrecy." His father had lowered his voice, inviting caution, and Peter spoke softly in reply.

"Are any of the others from school coming? Will Michael be there?"

"No, Peter. Only you."

"Why is that, Father?"

"You were appointed head of the Defense Club, you were just telling me," so his father had understood after all. "It will be up to you to lead the others where we're going. That's why I'm taking you tonight."

Peter's face was grave if there had been anyone to see it in the dark of the deserted town.

"So I want you to watch where you're going and remember how to get back if you have to. Later tonight you'll be taken to a certain part of the woods. I want you to know just where it is and how to get there without me or anyone else showing you."

"Yes, Father. I'll watch. I think I can remember."

"I know you can, Peter. You've spent a lot of your life in the woods. I'm counting on your woods sense to help."

They were now outside the town. The trail led north to Rabbit Mountain. In the dark Peter could see little of the track on which his skis slipped. But the hard tread told him it was a well-traveled path. They climbed with the aid of their poles and now and again would dig their runners into the hard snow banks to "walk up steps sidewise." But Peter and his father were well used to this kind of travel. They could talk as easily as if they were strolling in the town square.

"What did Uncle Victor mean about us going on our sleds to the Snake?" It was his first real chance to ask his father about the thing that was uppermost in his thoughts.

"Well, it's like this, Peter. There is a good deal of gold in Norway, more than we'd like to have fall into the hands of an enemy, especially one that might use it to make war on us. So we've decided to guard it with our lives. It isn't the gold itself so much. It's the fact that it may be used to bring death to the very people to whom it belongs."

"You're afraid of a German invasion, Father?"

"Well, that's the tale that Victor brought back from Oslo. When you came home and said he had returned, I knew that only one thing would bring him back at this time and that was that his country was in danger. But I didn't want you to know about it then. Today, however, other things have happened—foreign mine layers have been sighted off our coast. There is little use trying to hide something that may have to be faced."

"They're building air-raid shelters all over the south," Peter said.

"Yes, and they're taking other precautions, too. All this week a treasury official has been at the bank. He believes that the best way to safeguard our people is to put our wealth beyond the reach of those who would use it to do us harm. Other countries have been sending their gold to the United States for safe keeping. That's what we want to do, too, if it can be managed."

Peter could hardly believe this was real life and that it was he and his father who were talking and not two characters in a book or a film. His father was going on, and though his tones were the calm even ones of his ordinary speaking voice, Peter still had to struggle with a feeling of unreality.

"There may not be time to safeguard all the gold in the Bank of Norway this way," Mr. Lundstrom spoke confidentially. "To do so involves a good deal of care. Each of the places where the gold can be hidden has to be inspected by trusted people in the government. The treasury official came here first of all and had a long list of other places to visit. But even if he doesn't get to the other towns, good care will be taken of the rest of the money because it's a staggering sum, bullion worth hundreds of millions of kroner."

"And Uncle Victor will take it on his boat?" Peter asked.

"What we have here—if we can get it to the boat in time."

"So we are supposed to take it down the mountain on our sleds?"

"If there is an enemy in our country and there is no other way to get it out. You children would never be suspected, but the men wouldn't be allowed to load so much as a pound."

"But why don't you send it away before the enemy comes?"

"Because the British and French are mining our coasts, laying miles and miles of explosives in the sea. A ship that would stray in their direction would be blown to bits. So Uncle Victor has to wait until he can find out something about their location. Why, it would be suicide to sail until he does! That's why we have to hide the gold in the cave."

"Cave?" Peter blinked. "What cave?"

CHAPTER FIVE

PETER and his father reached a level stretch. Their trail paralleled a railroad siding that ended abruptly in the woods.

At one end of the track was a boxcar and on both sides of it were men and sleds. Peter could see only dark outlines against the snow for no light was showing. But when he got close he saw that a lantern was lit, its beams carefully shielded by the backs of the men.

One of the backs belonged to Uncle Victor.

"Hi, Lars," he greeted his brother cheerfully. "So you've brought Peter! Good!"

"He can help," his father said.

"He can go with Olsen. He's ready to leave. You can help him pull his sled, Peter."

His father turned to him. "Watch where Ole is taking you, Peter. That's the place you'll want to remember."

"Yes, Father." Peter gave a tug to the rope of the sled. It didn't move.

"Gee, it's heavy!"

"Heavy! I should say it is." Ole took up the rope. "It's a hundred and seventy thousand kroner. Your Uncle Victor would say forty thousand dollars."

Peter didn't care what Uncle Victor would say. "One hundred seventy thousand kroner in that sack!" He couldn't believe it.

They followed the railroad siding in the direction he and his father had come. Then they took a trail that led downhill for a distance. That made the going easier except where it was steep. There they had to hold the sled back to keep it from bumping their legs and knocking them forward down the slope. After a time they came to a dense part of the woods.

"Father said we were going to a cave," Peter asked Ole. "What cave?"

"Wait. You'll see."

Peter was mindful of his father's words to watch where he went and be able to return without help. Now he found he was recognizing landmark after landmark. Here was the rock they called The Ship when they played. There was the tree that was rotted through. When he was small, Per Garson told him that trolls lived in that tree, and to this day he thought of it as the trolls' tree. So he felt very much at home. Here he was in the woods he had known since babyhood, but in all his life he'd never heard of a cave there. That's why he was surprised when his father told him he would see one.

"We must be going a long ways off," he said. "I never heard of a cave anywhere near."

Ole grinned. "I guess you didn't," he said. "It's one we made ourselves."

"You made it?"

"Yes, you'll see."

They came to a high wall of snow. There they stopped. Ole led him past the wall and around its end. Now Peter could think of no part of the forest like this, where a wall stood as high as a man. And yet all the things near it were familiar, The Ship and the trolls' tree.

Then he guessed that the wall, like the cave, had been built by the men. When they drew the sled around it, he found himself blinking in the lights of lanterns and flashlights.

He was in a cave, indeed. In it were a dozen men and there was room for many more.

"You made it?" Peter was staggered.

"Not all," Ole explained. "Behind those stacks is a wall of stone that slopes so you could stand under it in a heavy rain and not get wet."

"I know. Thor's Rock. But it used to be open on every side."

"We closed it in with blocks of ice."

The men in the cave greeted Ole and Peter. Peter knew them all. There were Helga's father and Nanson, the sail maker, and Dr. Aker and Mr. Anders, the schoolmaster, among them. They were busy as beavers. The ones in the back did not stop for more than a nod to the newcomers. Three of the others rushed forward to remove the heavy brown sack from Ole's sled. Peter saw them rip it open and noted with surprise that it contained a number of smaller packages, each the size and shape of a building brick. These were counted carefully and listed on a paper Mr. Anders carried.

"Seventy-two, seventy-three, seventy-four," Dr. Aker was counting aloud. Later the doctor reached "thirteen hundred."

"Thirteen hundred of those bricks?" Peter asked Ole.

"Yes, and each of them contains eighteen and a half pounds of gold bullion—over twenty thousand kroner."

"It's a regular Aladdin's cave you're in," Nanson, the sail maker, spoke. "There aren't many boys who've been in a room with more than twenty-four thousand pounds of gold."

After a time some of the men Peter had seen at the railroad siding began coming in. With each arrival the same thing happened. The men in the cave would unload the sled, slit open the sack and begin counting and stacking the smaller packages it contained. Over them all hovered Mr. Anders with his paper and pencil.

"It's coming near the end." He smiled happily.

"Yes, praise all." Ole wiped his forehead.

"Tonight'll see the last." Nanson looked around from the wall he was making of the brick-sized packages.

"Here comes the rest of it," someone said as Uncle Victor and Peter's father came in together. "Every last pound's been removed."

"Does that make it come out all right, Anders?" Mr. Lundstrom asked.

The schoolmaster made a swift calculation. He looked at the sheets in his hand and counted the sleds to be unloaded. "Eighty-seven, eighty-eight. What have you there, Doctor?" he asked his helper. They quickly added the figures. "Well, Mr. Lundstrom," he announced proudly, "it's exactly right. It's all here."

CHAPTER SIX

THE NEXT night saw Norway blacked out from one end to the other. Over a thousand miles and not a light. Windows were draped in black and people were cautioned not to allow so much as a candle ray to show outside their houses.

That was the night of April eighth.

Throughout the country was the feeling of impending evil. It was as if some unknown terror would come out of the deep shadows.

Children who were old enough to know, cried themselves to sleep. But it was not alone they who were afraid. The grownups, too, saw fright in the black of night.

The air-raid shelters were hastily finished. Big blocks of ice served the purpose of sand bags in other countries.

In the houses were strange preparations. For what— no one could tell clearly. Hunting rifles were brought out and cleaned, though this was often unnecessary in that land of great hunters. Ancient pistols came out of hiding places, and clumsy fowling pieces were lifted down from pegs above doors.

Peter would have liked to go out to see what Riswyk looked like without a light anywhere. But that was impossible. Even though there was not yet a war, his father was leaving that night to join the regiment to which his class in military college belonged. Peter could not go out on his last night home.

"You're the man of the house, Peter," his father told

him. "You must look after your mother and the little ones."

Peter had expected to do this without being told.

"What about the gold?" he asked his father.

"Uncle Victor will tell you what to do. You may not need to do anything at all. There may be no trouble after all."

"But if there is? If there's a war?"

"You must wait for Uncle Victor. He'll tell you all you need to know. And though I know I don't have to warn you, not a word to anyone about what you're doing. If any stranger addresses you, you're to be deaf, dumb and blind. But you're not to talk."

"When do you suppose we'll start?"

"When Uncle Victor gives the word."

Peter thought this a most unsatisfactory answer. But he could see no good in asking further. If his father knew anything, clearly he wasn't going to tell.

Some of the men of Riswyk had already left town. Nanson, the sail maker, had gone and Michael Berg's father and many more. Mr. Anders, the schoolmaster, too. With him away, that day had been a holiday as would be the morrow and every other day. But what was the good of a holiday like that? No one wanted to play. They tried all the games they knew but no one seemed to enjoy any of them. Peter called a meeting of the Defense Club. The air-raid drill wasn't very exciting. For although they could blow a warning whistle, they had no one to give them the "All Clear" signal when to come out.

Helga and some of the girls thought it would be fun

to play at being Red Cross nurses. But when they picked Bunny for the first air-raid victim, he kicked and screamed so they had to let him go, even though his legs were supposed to be shot away.

But the long day dragged through somehow and now it was night. But what a different night, different from any Peter had ever lived through. He didn't know but what he would rather have a toothache.

After supper his father seemed to be waiting for some message. It never came. He kept taking his watch out to see the time although there were clocks everywhere you could look. His train did not go until midnight and the sleigh to take him to the station would not come for hours yet.

Peter peeped out of the window, careful that no light showed outside. There was nothing but darkness. There wasn't even a sound in this terrifying void. The world seemed to have come to an end at Peter's house. Life could not be possible in the blackness beyond.

When the hour finally came for Mr. Lundstrom to leave, they all tried to be cheerful. Peter's mother even started to make a little joke. Old Per Garson shuffled in for the bags and then the door closed and blotted out Peter's father in the black of the outside.

Mrs. Lundstrom turned to Peter in a flood of tears.

He tried to comfort her but there was little he could say.

"You've me, Mother. I'll not let anything happen to you. Father said I was to look after you and Lovisa and Bunny and I will."

She smiled when she spoke. "I know, Peter. I'm being foolish. After all, I *do* have you."

Four hours after that, German parachute troops landed in Norway, and through all the ports clear into the Arctic Circle, soldiers and marines poured out of merchant ships in the harbors. There were even grey-clad Nazi soldiers on the beach at Riswyk Fiord. It was Uncle Victor who brought the news in the morning.

"On your sleds, children," he directed. "There's not a day to lose."

CHAPTER SEVEN

"ARE N'T you in danger, Uncle Victor?" Peter asked. "Couldn't they take you prisoner?"

They were in the living room of Peter's home. Mrs. Lundstrom had taken Lovisa and Bunny and had gone to get some of the other children who were to help.

"Per Garson's on the watch. He'll tell me if anyone comes and I'll slip out the back and down the slope. They'll be good skiers to catch me."

"But they could shoot."

Uncle Victor only shrugged.

"Do you know where the British and French have laid their mines?" Peter hoped the answer would be yes. Otherwise what would be the use of taking the gold out of the cave if Uncle Victor couldn't sail away with it?

"Only partly."

"Well, why do we take the gold down the mountain if you can't sail away? I should think it'd be safer where it is."

"Peter, it's not right you should question anyone in authority," his uncle spoke irritably. "In military school you'll learn to do as you're told without asking why. But I'll tell you why it's important for you children to be seen on your sleds today. In the future, however, you're not to question."

"Yes, Uncle Victor," Peter spoke meekly. "You can't

sail the *Cleng Peerson* out of the Snake till you know where the mines are laid. But you can load her and have her ready to leave the minute you learn where they are. Is that the reason?"

"Not at all, Peter," his uncle answered. "The reason you must be on your sleds today near the fiord is to accustom the Germans to seeing you there. If they see you today and every day, they won't suspect anything unusual. But if, all at once, you started going in the direction of the Snake, they'd be stupid geese not to know something was going on."

Peter hadn't thought of that. How smart Uncle Victor was!

"Now about the mines," his uncle went on. "By the time the gold is loaded we'll know all we need to know about them. You don't suppose my fishermen can't find out anything they want to about our coast, do you? Remember, Peter, we're Norwegians and we're as much at home in the water as we are on land. This is our country and these are our waters and there's no foreign power that can keep us from using what's always belonged to us."

Victor Lundstrom thought he heard a noise. But it was not the heavy tread of marching men but the light quick steps of children, those who were to be seen on their sleds either around the town or down at the Snake. Today, only four of them would take gold to the Snake but after that there would be many more. Mrs. Lundstrom had gone first for Michael and Helga; and here they were, and Lovisa was with them.

"Now we can get started," Uncle Victor spoke. "Listen carefully while I tell you what you're to do. I may have to leave any minute so pay attention. If there's anything I miss, Fru Lundstrom or Per Garson will tell you."

There wasn't a sound from any of the four.

"What I'm going to say is of the gravest importance. On you, to an extent, depends the welfare of your country. If you do what you're told and do it right, you'll be helping countless Norwegians—not only the soldiers in the army but the people at home."

Eyes were bright at this mention of a chance to help their country.

"If you children win out, the enemy that today has invaded a peace-loving, unoffending country, will have less gold and so, fewer guns and less ammunition and food. Also, fewer opportunities to use our wealth to bring suffering and death to our people," he went on.

"Peter will take you to a place where we've hidden thirteen tons of gold bullion—money, you know, that's not been made into coins. Now, you are to take that bullion from its hiding place to the Snake where it will be loaded on my boat and taken to America to be kept safe for Norway.

"Here is what you do. Peter will take you to the hiding place. After that it's up to you. You'll have to find your own way back there later. What is more, you'll have to show the other children. So watch how you get there. Now in Riswyk School there are thirty-eight pupils, we think, old enough for this. These will divide into teams of nine, a captain and a squad of eight."

"That leaves two over," Peter spoke.

"Right," his uncle answered. "You and Michael will each have ten. Your mother has made up the teams. You four are captains and you must take the ones assigned to you, and no quarreling. And if any differences arise, Peter's the one to settle them. You must do as he says. Of course, your teams will split up on the way. You'll go in twos and threes. For if they counted nine and ten each time, they'd know something was up."

He stopped for a minute and then went on. "It's getting late and I've something very important to tell you. And that is, under no circumstances must you speak one word to a stranger. Not a syllable. Not so much as yes or no or good-day. Understand?"

The four of them nodded.

"Now today Peter will take you to the cave where we hid the gold. Per Garson will go along to load each sled. You'll each be given seventy-five pounds of bullion, that's over eighty thousand kroner, twenty thousand United States dollars. It will be packed in flat bricks and each of you will take four bricks. These you'll sit on or lie on when you ride 'belly-grinder.' "

"When you get to the Snake this afternoon you're to look for a place where there are two fallen trees. They are pretty well buried under the snow, but you'll find them because you're Norwegians. You know such things. Between these trees you're to bury your bricks in the snow. Over the top of each pile you'll build a snowman. When I come out at night with Rolls, my mate, I'll only have to find the snowmen."

This was even better than playing pirates, Peter decided.

"Now about the return trip. You start back up the mountain to the Holms' farm where you'll spend the night. They have room for dozens. The girls will stay in the house and the boys in the barn. You will get a warm supper and breakfast next day. Then you'll come back here. But it won't matter if you are late because you are to rest that day and start back to the Snake the next day. The way we've planned it is for two teams to go one day and the two others the next. That will give you a day to rest up, or almost a day."

Per Garson stuck his head in the door.

"Jan from the sailyard comes," he said. "He thinks the Germans are starting up the mountain."

Uncle Victor jumped up.

"Oh, Uncle Victor, don't let them get you," Lovisa moaned.

He slipped out of the room and through the kitchen to the outside. They could hear the whiz of his skis on the hard snow.

CHAPTER EIGHT

"WELL, what are we waiting for?" Michael asked. "You know the way to this cave or whatever it is." He turned to Peter. "What's wrong with going there and getting this thing started?"

Uncle Victor had left because he had been warned the Germans were on their way to Riswyk. Per Garson had shown him out and the children were alone in the room. They could hear nothing after the sound of his skis had died away.

"Right." Peter jumped up. "We're supposed to be seen near the beach today so we'll have to get started. But first there's something we should do before we begin any of this. I think we ought to make a pact we'll never tell anything if we're caught."

"We won't get caught," Michael spoke.

"But if we are?"

"Bah!" he shook his crew-cut hair.

"I still think we should make a pact we won't tell one word about what we're doing, about taking gold to the Snake."

"We'd hardly do that after what your Uncle Victor said about not so much as a word to strangers." Helga Thomsen was scornful that Peter thought such a promise necessary.

"But if we're tortured? If they try to make us tell, and

torture us if we don't?" Michael's eyes shone with excitement. "What if they threaten to pull out our tongues if we don't tell?"

"Not if our tongues were to be pulled out would we tell!" Helga shook her black curls.

"There'd be little sense in that if they really wanted us to talk." Lovisa could always see the funny side.

"Then you wouldn't mind swearing?" Peter ignored Lovisa's interruption. "If you're sure you wouldn't tell, you wouldn't mind pledging yourselves."

"Certainly I wouldn't mind swearing," Helga answered. "No matter how I was tortured, I'd not say a word."

Peter went to the fireplace and climbed on a chair to bring down a sword his ancestors had used in wars against the Swedes, hundreds of years before. He drew off its dried leather cover.

"Swear on this then. Hands on the blade."

"I swear." Helga put her hand on the wide blade and Lovisa and Michael put theirs beside hers.

"I swear." Lovisa's blue eyes were round.

"I swear I'll have my tongue pulled out. I'll be tortured with a red-hot poker, and I'll have my head on a pole before I'll say a single word," Michael spoke excitedly.

"And I the same." Peter put back the sword. "Now we'd better be off to the cave for our loads. It's just us today. Tomorrow or the next day we will take the others."

"Should we make them swear, too?" Michael asked.

"What's the use? They'll know they're not to talk to strangers."

"But maybe we should make them swear."

"After what Uncle Victor said in school? About obeying without a question? I guess not." Peter had great faith in his uncle. When he gave a command it was obeyed. "Come on. Let's be going."

"Beat you to the sleds," Helga spoke.

There was a scramble for the door. On the way, buttons were done up and zippers made magic silver seams down the fronts of windbreakers that had been loosened when the children came indoors.

"Per Garson," Peter remembered. "He's to be at the cave to load the sleds."

He ran to the kitchen to look for him. He was not

there. Peter opened the kitchen door. Outside on the snow he saw a strange sight.

Per Garson was racing madly around and around on skis. Old and bent, he was nevertheless skiing with the grace of an Olympic entrant. He swooped and sailed. He would loop and then would take off in a jump. Peter thought he had lost his senses. Then he saw there was a design in the crazy pattern he was making in the snow.

"He's covering Uncle Victor's tracks," he guessed. For Per had already been down the slope and had made cat steps all the way down to the hollow at its base.

"We're going now, Per Garson," he called.

"Ja, I go, too." He made a mad leap and landed exactly at Peter's side. "I see you by the woods. You know how to go? Sure?" Then he gave a solemn wink, his old eyes screwed in his brown wrinkled face.

Peter had not the least doubt where to go. He told Per Garson so.

"Is good. I see you there." He gave another long leap and began a long swift flight through the churned snow.

Peter raced around to the front to get his sled.

"What'd you do if you met a German right here?" Michael tried to frighten the girls.

"I'd do just what I'm doing now." Helga's eyes flashed. "I'd go on without so much as a look at him," she sniffed.

They all knew the way to Thor's Rock, so Peter found he wasn't much needed as a guide. Never mind. After they got there he'd have to show them how to go around the wall of snow into the cave.

They trudged through the woods taking all possible

short cuts. When they got to Thor's Rock and the place where the cave had been, Peter got the surprise of his life.

There was no cave.

CHAPTER NINE

PETER was sure he had not been mistaken. But here was Thor's Rock and there was no cave anywhere that he could see.

There had been a high wall of snow in front if it, he remembered. But look as he would, all he could see were young pines.

"Ole said it was where the rock curved so you could stand in a heavy rain and not get wet. That's here," he told the others. But for all they searched they could find neither wall nor cave.

It was Lovisa who spied Per Garson's brown face framed in the branches of a young fir.

"You said you could get here without help," he teased Peter when they came close. "It's here all the time."

"There weren't any trees the other night." Peter felt ashamed. He had been so sure he knew just where to find the cave but he had to be shown after all.

"These we fixed to make it seem more real," Per Garson explained. When Peter looked again he saw that a strip of evergreens made a narrow corridor in front of the wall.

"You made it since the night I was here—since the night before last?"

"Ja. Ole and some others. They came yesterday and finished before the blackout."

Peter was still unbelieving. But sure enough, behind the trees was the wall of snow and back of that the cave.

Per Garson led them around shrubbery to the entrance.

"Shouldn't someone stand guard over the door in case the Germans come?" Helga asked. "I'll do it."

"Is no need, I think," Per Garson answered. "Still— is no harm to watch. Spies are everywhere."

So Helga posted herself behind the tree where Per Garson had been waiting and the others went into the cave.

There was a strange kind of white light inside. Peter thought it might be like being in one of the sepulchres of the Bible. For the strong sunlight was cut down by the wall in front of the doorway and a pearly beam fell on the sides and floor.

Per Garson went at once to the end where a stack of brown bricks rose up like a garden wall.

"Gold," Peter whispered to Michael.

"That? Gold?" Peter agreed with Michael that it was hard to believe that each of those brown bricks was money enough to buy an airplane.

Per Garson began lifting down the bricks.

He laid four of them, side by side, on Peter's sled. Then he went to the far side of the cave to a pile of rough brown sacks like potato sacks—the bags that had covered the bricks on their journey to the cave. He carried one of these to Peter's sled. He folded it twice and laid it over the rectangle of bricks.

"Next the rope." He produced a new clothesline and with it began lashing the sack and bricks to the sled. Over and over went the rope. Then he drew out a long knife and cut the clothesline.

44

"We could help you, Per Garson," Peter suggested. "Then we could start sooner."

"Na, this must be done right."

"We could do it right."

"Na. Na. Your Uncle Victor holds me to blame if anything goes wrong. He says we can't have the rope coming loose and the bricks falling in the snow. One time for that and the Germans would have our gold."

They watched him take down more bricks for the next sled. Then more for the next and the next. For an old man he worked quickly. With each sled, the same procedure. First the bricks, then the sack folded twice, then the clothesline.

"Now you tell Helga to come here. I think we can be safe these few minutes."

Michael went to get Helga. She had seen nothing more than a few squirrels.

"Now I show you how to untie the rope," Per Garson announced. "When you get to the Snake you first look for a pair of trees that are fallen and covered with snow. They're 'bout two hundred feet apart. Be sure you find them for that's the place your uncle thinks is safest. Now you untie the knots. And so. And so!"

"Can you do it? Try." He laced the bricks onto the sled again and Peter tried to untie them. He was clumsy at first. Instead of openings he made knots. But after a time he learned how to untie the rope.

When it came Helga's turn she gave one quick pull and the rope was dangling from her hand.

"Good. You learn things fast," Per Garson praised.

Each of them had to prove he knew how to unload

45

the sleds. Michael was slower than Peter to learn. He tried again and again and each time succeeded only in making the knots tighter.

"Never mind." Peter was anxious to get started. "I'll untie his for him."

"Na, he'll have to know. Next time he'll have to show his team."

The lesson went on and after a time Michael learned the trick.

"And can you show the others?"

Michael felt he could.

"All right, then. Off with you. You bring back the ropes and sacks. These we need again," Per Garson instructed. "For your pockets, here." He handed each a flat parcel. "Your lunch. For supper you go to Holms' farm where you'll get plenty good hot meal."

He led the way to the opening. "Now I think it's time you go."

CHAPTER TEN

SOON would come the moment the four children dreaded—the first German sentry.

Per Garson said the Nazis were on their way to the town but the children had not seen them.

The rest of the morning had been spent pulling the heavy sleds through the woods. They had to go almost all the way back to Riswyk before they could begin to toboggan down the mountain.

What would happen?

What if the Nazis refused to allow them to go on?

What if, somehow, they suspected and began to search the sled?

Peter wouldn't let himself think of what might happen. He made up stories about the four of them. They were Vikings and their sleds were Viking boats. They were sailing the seas. They would go far, far away. The very nearest they would go would be to America.

"Peter, I'm hungry. Let's eat," Michael proposed when they were barely out of the woods. But Peter had wanted to get a start on the long ride down the mountain. When Michael repeated his request a little later he agreed.

It's an idea, he thought. It would postpone their first brush with the sentinels.

"Girls, we eat," Michael yelled.

They pulled up on a bank beside the road. Their sleds

in a cluster, they sat munching the dark bread, dried fish, cheese and cold meat.

"Come on, Michael. Race you to the lookout." Peter wiped his mouth on the back of his mitten.

The lookout was where Peter and Michael, Helga and Lovisa had seen Uncle Victor the day he had so strangely returned to Norway. But now, when the four companions reached that point, it was not to be the scene of a snow battle and all the fun that went with it. Instead there were solemnness and silence, and Lovisa's blue eyes were round with fright.

The lookout today revealed an entirely different sight and one to strike fear into the stoutest.

A German freighter was at anchor in the fiord. Steaming up, she might be about to sail. On the beach that lay between the Atlantic Ocean and Riswyk Fiord, there were hundreds of grey-clad soldiers and there were others on the narrow strip of land between the big fiord and the small one they called the Snake. They were unloading enormous supplies because the snow was covered with bales, boxes, crates and drums. Rifles were stacked in neat rows, and up and down the beach in front of the fishing pier, sentries were goose-stepping while their companions worked.

"Whew!" Peter drew off his cap to wipe his forehead.

And now Lovisa was not the only one to be afraid. Fear looked out of all eyes.

It was Helga who made them brave again.

"I'm not afraid of any goose step!" She shook the curls that hung like sausages from under her hood. "What's there to be afraid of?"

"Come on, then." Peter straightened his shoulders. He drew his sled away from the others. "Let's go."

"Look!" Michael could not take his eyes off the beach. "Soldiers marching right up our sled track. How'll we get down?"

They turned back to the sight below. Michael was right. A company of men had started up the only road that led from the sea to the mountain.

"We could hide till they passed," Lovisa urged.

"Or go down over the rocks," Michael suggested.

"But what'd we do with our sleds? We couldn't take them down that way," Peter replied.

"We'll have to meet them sometime," Helga said. "It might as well be now as later."

"Right," Peter answered. "Uncle Victor said they were to see us today on our sleds. If we sail right into them they'll see us for sure. Come on. Keep to the side and try not to spill any of 'em for that'd be bad for us."

He fell face down on his sled. With a shove he began the descent to the beach.

The Germans were a long way off. The road made several turns in the miles between the lookout and the shore below and only from the lookout could any part of the road be seen. So there was no way to tell if the Germans would turn off before they met them.

"Maybe they're not coming all the way," Peter told himself. "Maybe they'll turn aside."

But when he rounded the slope's last bend he had no such hope. Directly in front was a company of grey-clad, goose-stepping soldiers. Even on the glassy surface their legs swung out straight as rods.

Peter had no way to stop himself and now he found he was headed right into the middle of them. He let out a war whoop, a warning he was coming. But the Germans were directly in his path. He didn't see how he could avoid knocking them down like ten pins.

He was going to spill them, all right, try as he might not to. It was the worst possible thing, he knew. Near at hand these grim grey marching soldiers towered like giants to the boy on his sled.

Down he flew, faster, faster.

At one hundred yards he swerved toward the bank to avoid knocking down a whole row of men.

A voice was barking a command in German and the company took three steps to the side and out of Peter's path.

His swerve drove him into the bank and stopped him as he had not dared to hope. But he had already passed

the first of the troops. Only their quick side march had saved a collision.

He raised his eyes from the snow. He was looking into the smiling face of a German infantry captain.

"I turn my men aside." He spoke in Norwegian. "It is not right that we spoil your sledding. When I was a boy I liked nothing better than sledding."

CHAPTER ELEVEN

THE BLOOD rushed out of Peter's head. He was certainly dizzy. He closed his eyes. When he opened them again he was looking up the slope at the heels of the last row of German goose-steppers.

Michael and the girls joined him on the bank.

"Well, what do you know about that?" Michael was open-eyed with wonder.

"He turned his whole company aside!" Lovisa found it equally hard to believe.

Peter sat up. "If he hadn't, I would have plowed right into 'em. I might have broken my sled and the bricks would have spilled, maybe."

"The least that could have happened would have been to make them angry." Helga spoke thoughtfully.

"We've been lucky, I guess," Peter admitted.

"I told you there was nothing to be afraid of." Helga shook her curls. "When they turn out for you like that they can't be so terrible. Come on. We've got to get to the Snake."

There were more German soldiers to pass before they could make the bend into the farther fiord they called the Snake. To these they would likewise have to come close.

Nearest were the sentries that patrolled between the stacked rifles and the road down from the mountains. The sleds would pass within a few feet of where they walked.

"If Uncle Victor wants them to see us today he gets what he wants," Lovisa pointed out. "They'd have to be blind to miss us."

"Uncle Victor didn't know it would be as bad as this," Peter grumbled. "He didn't say they'd be marching on the road."

"Well, we got past them, didn't we? Come on. Peter, let me go first," Helga begged. "It would look even less suspicious if a girl went first."

But Peter was head of the Defense Club and it was for him to lead them wherever they had to go. No matter what would happen, he must go first. But he was still frightened enough to want Helga to take the lead.

On their sleds again, and the last mile before they would turn the bend by the cliff that hid the entrance to the Snake.

The sentries were taking their stiff-kneed walks beside the rifles. The other Germans went on with their work of unloading the supplies. Nobody so much as looked at the children on their sleds.

What if the sentries were to stop them? Peter asked himself. What if they wouldn't let them pass?

The captain had been friendly because he himself used to like to toboggan, and anyway it was not his job to be on watch as it was these guards'.

But when he went directly in front of the first sentry, he saw only a blank face. There was not so much as a look to show if he was pleased or displeased.

Beyond the sentry Peter saw some soldiers dragging a heavy tarpaulin over the snow. One of them looked in his direction. Under the round cap and fringe of yellow

hair he saw the bluest eyes he had ever seen in his life. They seemed to say that he, too, would like to be sled riding.

Another sentry was stepping up the line over the churned snow and beyond him, another. Like the first one, they had only blank looks to give the children. None of them so much as lifted a finger to stop them.

So they were going to be allowed to go on!

Uncle Victor had been right when he said that no one would suspect boys and girls on their sleds.

Peter breathed a sigh of relief and dug his heels into the snow for a fresh start.

The cliff that hid the Snake was just ahead. Beyond it they would be safe from curious eyes. That day, anyway, would be won.

The sleds would have to be dragged the rest of the way as the ground was level. But it wasn't far to go, after the cliff was passed. There only remained to find the two fallen trees and to bury the gold and build the snowmen.

In the Snake, Peter stopped to get his breath. His sled was terribly, terribly heavy. He hadn't noticed how heavy it was when he pulled it through the woods from the cave. Now it was a fearful load.

The others were close on his heels. They, too, seemed tired. Even Helga crept along, dragging her crushing load of gold.

"But where's Uncle Victor's boat?" Peter searched both sides of the stream with his eyes. There was no boat on the black water.

"The trees!" Lovisa's eyes fell on a flat stretch that was closed in at two ends by long ridges of snow.

"Here's one of them." She poked her arm to the elbow into the crusted white. Then she ran through the deep untrodden stretch. "And here," she called, "is the other."

The four of them began burrowing in the snow. Four pits were made and into each went the brown-covered bricks. Then four snowmen rose over the bricks. Each stood guard over a mound of gold worth more than eighty thousand kroner—twenty thousand dollars. So, between the trees, eighty thousand dollars in gold bullion lay buried in the snow.

"We've done it!" Peter exulted. "We passed them and they never guessed."

"Dumb stupid things." Helga's lips curled in scorn.

"We did it! We did it!" Lovisa thumped Helga on the back and then threw her arms around Peter.

And now none of them was tired. They pounded one another's backs and shoulders. They joined hands and circled around and around Peter's snowman.

"And the captain turned aside his troops because he didn't want to spoil our sled track!" Helga burst out laughing. "Oh, if he only knew!" Tears ran out of her eyes. Weak from laughter she could no longer stand and fell helplessly in the snow.

In roars the others fell down beside her.

"He said when he was a boy, there was nothing he liked better than sledding!" Peter choked with mirth. "He likes sledding and so do we."

"Oh, if he only knew!"

CHAPTER TWELVE

PETER would have liked to tell Uncle Victor about the events of that day. But Uncle Victor and his boat were nowhere to be seen.

It was strange, for Peter knew the *Cleng Peerson* was somewhere in the Snake. But look where he would, all he could see was the black rushing water, the bobbing ice cakes and the snow that covered ground and trees alike.

It was getting late. They had to get to the Holms' farm before the blackout. It was three miles up the road from the beach. They'd have to hurry.

It was twilight by the time the little band turned into the farmyard. Here, they were on familiar ground.

They'd passed the German sentries a second time. Again they saw the friendly captain who had turned aside his soldiers. He was returning with his troops and he greeted them.

"Did you have a good sled ride?" he asked in excellent Norwegian.

Peter was sorry he wasn't allowed to answer him.

At the farm kitchen Michael pounded on the door.

"Who is it?" a frightened voice called out.

When Michael gave their names there was a scuffle inside. They had to be recognized before the door would be opened.

"But come in, come in," the farmwife called. And Peter thought that for all the sadness of that terrible day, there was still a cheerfulness about the good brown face. That they had succeeded in carrying the gold past the Nazi sentries seemed to bring hope for Norway.

"You had no trouble?" Her husband came out of a dim corner.

Their supper was even now being dished into great earthenware bowls. Peter thought he had never smelled anything so good. Nor had he seen anything for a long time as pleasant as the flickering dancing light from the fire and from the candles on the dresser and great long kitchen table.

"First they eat, Papa. Then they talk." Fru Holm and her servant bustled back and forth between the fire and the table. "Draw up now and eat, you brave children. You must be famished."

Great steaming dishes dotted the red-and-white-checkered cloth—meat, potatoes, dumplings, cabbage. On the table were also many cold foods, dried herrings, pickled eggs, mackerel and great round sheets of the hard rye *knackebrod*. Also huge mounds of iced cookies.

The children fell upon the food like puppies around a basin of milk. It disappeared like snow when brought into the house. Fru Holm and Marie, the servant, were kept busy walking back and forth between the table and the stove refilling the bowls. Herr Holm sat in a rocking chair, his pipe between his teeth.

"So you got through all right?" The rough old farmer could not wait to hear their story.

"Papa, let them eat," his wife kept urging. "When Marie and I are washing up you shall hear."

"Ja. Ja. Eat your fill," he rocked contentedly. "It's

wonderful that we have boys and girls like these who can trick the Germans and not get caught." He chuckled.

"Shhhh, Papa. Spies everywhere," Fru Holm cautioned. "Could be even here."

Peter drew a long sigh of satisfaction. Never before had he felt so content. The warm food sent a glow to every part of his body.

"We fooled them, all right," he boasted. "They even turned out of our way. The captain said they didn't want to spoil our sledding."

With that, the four of them went into spasms of laughter. The tears rolled down Lovisa's face. Michael had to hold his stomach after all that food.

"But what is so funny?" their host inquired. "Tell us so we can laugh, too. You fooled them, but what is funny?"

The four of them started talking at once. But they kept interrupting themselves to laugh. They started to tell of Peter's ride down the mountain, head on in the path of the German army corps. Then they all had to stop because they were choking. So it was some time before poor Herr Holm could make out what had happened. But when he learned of the politeness of the captain whose only fear was that he might spoil their sled track, he, too, shouted with laughter.

They told him all that had happened, even to Lovisa's finding the fallen trees.

"But Uncle Victor's boat! It's not there." Peter was serious.

"You find the trees but not the boat," Herr Holm chided. "That's because your uncle wishes it so."

"You mean he sailed away?"

"Na. Na. In the last war, things were hidden by what was called camouflage. What it's called today, I do not know. You cover well with branches of trees or with snow or whatever. Even from the air you couldn't tell."

Herr Holm would have kept the children talking all night if his wife had let him.

"To bed with them. Their eyes are buttoned with sleep."

Peter remembered being led from the house to the barn but was aware of nothing else. The next thing he knew it was morning.

"Wake up, my little soldiers," the farmer was saying. "Hours ago I came by and did my milking and you heard not a sound."

Peter was grumpy at being aroused.

"But would you sleep till noon?" Herr Holm asked in surprise. "You have work to do."

Peter murmured, "Why do we have to be in such a hurry? We can get past those sentries any time."

"Ja, if the snow holds," Herr Holm spoke anxiously.

In alarm Peter jumped up.

"If the snow holds!"

CHAPTER THIRTEEN

A LL THAT week and all the next there was a steady stream of children and sleds down the mountains. And every sled carried gold, sometimes as much as would equal twenty thousand American dollars.

Each morning saw a band of children trudging through the woods to the cave where the gold had been hidden a bare few days before the German invasion. By noon, the Norse children were well on their way to the Snake to bury their loads beneath the snow.

Always the same thing happened. Part way down the mountain came the stop for lunch. From pockets came the flat packages Per Garson had provided. Then the lookout and a sight of the invaders on the beach.

But the view from the lookout was very different from the one Peter and his friends had seen the day the Germans had come to Norway. The freighter had steamed out to sea and had disappeared. Out of the turmoil of unloading had come a little city. Long barracks rose up at the foot of the fishing pier. There were other orderly buildings to house equipment and supplies.

The children began to recognize some of the Germans. Peter often saw the blue-eyed private who looked, that first day, as if he, too, would like to be sled riding. Then there was the captain who had turned his troops out of the path of Peter's sled. But him they saw no longer. He seemed to have gone away. There was a new

Commandant and the tales about him that reached Riswyk were enough to make the blood run cold.

There was now no doubt about passing the sentries. The children knew in advance they would not be stopped. Not even the fierce new Commandant had thought to tell his pickets to challenge them.

The Germans still tried to make friends with the children. But now as before, they were met with silence. Cakes of chocolate were offered as bribes, but the venture ended its third week and not a single Norwegian child had said as much as "Hello" to any of the Nazi soldiers.

The four friends had separated after that first day. Each had his own team and they met only when they passed on the road or two of them met at the cave or the Snake or when the day ended at the Holms' farm. Peter's team and Helga's would go out the same day

and Michael's team and Lovisa's the following morning.

For the first time in the history of Riswyk, no one wanted to see spring come. Warm weather would bring the end of the snow and stop the sled trips. That far in the north the snow lasted well into May, sometimes late May. But the thaws could come any time now and, indeed, were looked for since winter had set in so early.

"If the snow holds" was the one thought in all the town. "Could it stay long enough to get the whole thirteen tons of bullion to the Snake?"

Well, it was an unusual year, everyone seemed to say. Never before had the snow been so deep. Not even Granny Gohla, who was ninety, remembered anything like it.

"Will the snow hold?" the townspeople asked each other.

"Will it hold?" Per Garson rubbed his whiskered chin thoughtfully. He looked at the sky and smelled the air and looked at the very snow itself.

"Do you think it will last, Granny Gohla?" he asked.

"Ja, I think it will," she answered brightly. It made him feel better, he told Peter.

Three weeks of hard, hard sledding for the children and what was the result? Back in the cave Per Garson looked ruefully at the big stacks of bricks that remained. Why they seemed hardly to have made a hole in them!

"How much more?" Peter kept asking him.

Well, he was no Mr. Anders, the schoolmaster. But as well as he could count, it would take another three weeks, maybe longer, to empty the cave.

They hadn't been able to do all they expected. The

smaller children couldn't pull the loads that Peter and Michael and the bigger boys could haul. The sleds had to be dragged on the level stretches of the woods and down on the beach. The girls had to take fewer bricks. Lovisa who, after all, was only ten, had been too tired after that first day and now she carried two bricks where she had taken four. But Helga insisted she was strong as any boy and not one brick would she give up.

If all had gone as the grownups planned, most of the gold would have been taken down those first few weeks. They'd counted on moving four tons a week. But that was expecting every child to take four bricks or seventy-five pounds on every sled load. But there were less than a dozen who could do that. Instead of four tons, they were averaging only a little over two tons a week.

"Well, it can't be helped," Per Garson sighed. But three whole weeks were gone and the snow must melt sometime. "If I only dared do it myself," Peter heard him moan.

That day the sun showed itself not once. There was not the faintest streak of brightness in the dishwater grey of the sky. The wind had died out without a trace of breeze, even off the sea.

Without the sun, it ought to have been cold, Peter knew. But he had had to open his lumber jacket as he pulled his sled home from Holms' farm.

Helga was cross and tired and the two had quarreled about which of them had been first at the Holms' pump. The quarrel was odd because Helga was ordinarily too busy to bother about such things and Peter was known throughout the town for his even disposition.

It was funny how as little a thing as the weather could disturb a whole day, he reflected as he lagged his way into the town.

At home Per Garson complained of his bones aching. "I don't need any almanac to tell me when there'll be a change in the weather," he said.

"A change in the weather!" Peter's voice sounded high and excited. "What sort of change?"

But Per Garson only shook his grey head and said nothing.

After supper Per went out to bring in the kindling. He threw a big log on the fire. The curtains were drawn for the blackout. Their dark heavy folds showed not the tiniest brightness, not even a glint of reflection from the fire. The northern day had lengthened. It should have been twilight. So the darkness outside was all the more forbidding.

Mrs. Lundstrom was knitting in the light of a lamp. With a shade, especially designed for the blackout, the lamp cast a gloomy look, rather than brightness. Peter felt his mother's thoughts must be far away for she had not even looked up when Per Garson came in with the log.

Per raked up the ashes and soon had a fine fire. The wood burst into flame and to Peter, the whole room seemed livelier for its dancing light. But it blew a hot gusty breath into the corner where Mrs. Lundstrom sat.

"But, Per, we don't need so big a fire!" she rebuked

him gently. "Why, it's hot enough in here to bake bread."

"I'm sorry," the old man mumbled. "I guess I'm just plain absent-minded these days. My rheumatism bothers me and I forget." He shuffled out, the fire tongs still in his hands.

Peter went to the kitchen to get a drink of water. Per was busy locking the house for the night. When he had finished he came back to the kitchen and carefully shielding the light so it would not be seen outside, peered through the window. But there was nothing to be found out about this blackness. He stepped out of doors.

Peter followed him. He sensed more trouble or sorrow in the old man and he tried to find words of comfort. He thought Per was ashamed at having been so careless as to build a big fire.

"Don't mind about that," he said. "Mother doesn't really mind."

"Heh? What's that?" Per seemed aware of Peter for the first time.

"About the fire. Wood's plentiful. What if you did build a big fire? It makes no difference, 'cept it's too hot."

"Oh, that," Per seemed to shrug. It was so dark that neither of them could see the other. Per Garson shoved out his hand and in doing so struck Peter smartly on the shoulder. Peter hardly knew what to make of the sudden blow, especially when no apology or explanation followed. Clearly Per Garson had no intention of including the young master in what was going on in his busy mind.

But when next he spoke, Peter knew why he had been accidentally struck. Per Garson had only stretched forth his hand and in doing so had hit Peter. But he found out what he wanted to know. He only spoke one word but that word spelled catastrophe.

"Rain," he said.

CHAPTER FOURTEEN

RAIN. But that couldn't be.

Why it would spoil everything.

The children couldn't go down to the Snake with their bricks of gold if the rain melted the snow and spoiled their sled track.

And now Peter felt it was more important than anything else for him to go to the Snake tomorrow. He had complained to himself of the long tiring trip. He said he despised the same dull journey, every second day. But he also knew that more than anything else in the world, he wanted the bullion delivered to the Snake.

Though the snow was ten feet deep in drifts and hard packed on all the trails, a heavy rain would finish the sled rides. The mountain itself would be turned into a cataract. One could be swept along and could even be drowned in the raging rush of water.

"It could be snow," Peter told Per Garson.

"No. Rain," the servant said flatly. "See for yourself."

But Peter had no need to stretch out his hand for the raindrops. They were on his hair and in his face. The rain had begun to fall steadily and was making a pelting sound on the hard crusted snow.

He followed Per Garson back to the house, uncertain whether or not he should worry his mother with news of this new turn of events.

Inside the kitchen they could hear the steady downpour on the roof of the one story lean-to.

When Peter went back to the living room, the rain was pounding against the windows. It could be heard through the panes of the double storm glass. No need to be afraid of telling his mother. Her look said that the rain could only be regarded as a calamity.

"It does seem a shame." Her head was bent over her knitting. "We've had trouble enough. And now this—".

"But what will we do, Mother?"

"I don't know. We'll just have to wait and see. Perhaps Uncle Victor can help us out. He may be able to think of a way if the sleds can no longer be used."

"Uncle Victor? Why his boat's not there! I've looked for it every time and I've not seen it once."

"Oh, I think it's there, all right, Peter. I don't think we'll have any trouble finding it if we need to."

"Well, I hope you're right," Peter sighed. "I looked for it and so did Helga. Helga has eyes that can see through a wall, almost—but we've never once seen it."

Mrs. Lundstrom's busy fingers flew in and out of the wool. The fire flickered and burned more brightly.

Lovisa was putting Bunny to bed. She always told him a story before he went to sleep. Ordinarily the sound of her voice, and sometimes his, would be heard in the living room. But tonight the storm shut out everything but itself.

The rain kept drumming down. When Lovisa came in to say good night, it seemed less heavy. There was a new noise outside.

The wind seemed to have caught up with its sleep and to have shaken off the stupor that had held it all day. Now it blew a loud roar. It tried to get into the house that had been well sealed against the northern winter. The only entrance was by the chimney and down that it came with a shower of sparks that blew out on the rug. Peter was kept busy stamping them out.

Per Garson came in to bank the fire before he would go to bed. Instead of his slow shuffling gait, there was a new sprightliness to him.

"Use some of the liniment for your rheumatism," Mrs. Lundstrom said. "I'll rub it in for you."

"Is no need, I think."

Another great blow drove a gust of hot air out into the room. Per Garson's thick-soled shoes stomped up and down beating out the big ember that had blown almost across to the blackout curtains.

"I fetch a screen for the hearth," he spoke gleefully.

"Perhaps it would be safer if you put the fire out," Mrs. Lundstrom suggested.

"Oh, but the cold. You'd die of the cold in the morning. But don't worry, I fix it so neither the house burns down nor you freeze to death."

Mrs. Lundstrom put down her knitting.

"Why, Per Garson," she looked up, smiling, "I believe you know something."

"Ja, my bones. They tell me when there'll be a change in the weather. The rain turns to snow, my shoulder says. By midnight, all will be as you've never seen it, something you've not seen in your time." He spoke happily but there was just a trace of scorn in his tone. It was scorn for all who had not lived as many years as he. "Tomorrow you will see something you know nothing about. For this late in April—a blizzard!"

Per Garson was right.

The next morning the world was a raging white fury.

The Lundstrom house rocked through the night as the storm battered and pounded and pummeled. The wind seeped in through the tight fitting double windows. It entered through cracks and crevices that no one knew existed. It seemed to force its way through openings that had been puttied and sealed with the greatest care. It tossed ancient ashes of the many fireplaces into little whirlpools of dust in all the rooms. By morning the kitchen had a spread of gritty black dirt over its usually spotless boards.

But the Lundstroms slept soundly that night. Now they could hope for the gold's safe transit again.

There was no question of going to the Snake or anywhere else in the morning. Not even the weather-brave Norse children could venture out in such a storm. For three days the people of Riswyk kept to their homes. The postman seemed to be a person of the past. No one knew what had become of him. On the third day of the blizzard, Dr. Aker started out to see one of his sick. But the way he walked backward in the wind and battled to keep his coat from being blown off, and dug his sealskin earmuffs into the collar of his coat, was enough to make people turn back to their own fires with a feeling of thankfulness that they didn't have to go out.

There was food aplenty in all the houses. No one needed to worry about a neighbor going hungry. And though the kindling seemed to be eaten up by the hungry fire-breathing dragons of the hearths, none in Riswyk would lack wood if the blizzard lasted a week.

But what of the Germans? How were they standing this storm, the like of which only the very old could remember?

Well, what of the Germans? Nothing could be done for them anyway. And since nobody had invited them to come up to the Arctic Circle to share a Norway blizzard, they would have to manage the best they could. Their buildings were erected hurriedly and without the many inventive devices the Norwegians used to secure their own homes against the cold.

"If their barracks blow over, they'll be good and mad," Lovisa chuckled. She was enjoying being snowbound as was every member of the Lundstrom household including Bunny who had missed his brother and sister on their trips away from home. Now he was overjoyed to be the center of attention again. He had been almost adored and was close to being spoiled before the Germans came to Norway. Since then, Peter and Lovisa played with him only when they had time and were not too tired. In some way that Bunny didn't quite understand, he knew it was the Germans who interfered with his fun. Now it was the same as before they came.

So Bunny was happy and so was the rest of the household. But the happiest of all was Per Garson.

His bones? Why they must have felt like a kitten's. He went about his tasks with light quick steps. His stooped shoulders straightened whenever he wasn't carrying heavy armloads of wood or bringing in rugs or blankets to cover cracks where the snow came whirling in. Yes, Per Garson was in fine spirits.

"But you've seen nothing at all!" he kept saying. "If

you don't remember the blizzard of eighty-nine, you don't know what cold weather is. Why this is nothing but a cold snap!"

Mrs. Lundstrom had to laugh. "This is bad enough for me, Per, and I guess, for everyone else."

Peter thought he would go out to the kitchen to read the barometer. They were all eager to know what to expect of the weather on the morrow.

"What's the use?" Lovisa drawled. "Just ask Per Garson. Per, what do your bones say?"

"My bones say you stop mocking!" He shook his fist at her.

CHAPTER FIFTEEN

THE NEW snow was a sparkling white sheet that spread over everything.

The windows of the houses had shaggy white eyebrows and the doors were all but blocked up with dense woolly beards.

The sunlight scattered handfuls of diamonds over the streets. In the yards were crystal prisms that showed every color of the rainbow where the sun touched the glittering white.

Throughout Riswyk was a flurry of snow shoveling the day the blizzard subsided. It commenced from almost the earliest light.

On the way to the cave, Peter found the snow knee-deep in places. He would sink into it but his light sled rode on top or would drop but a few inches below the crest. His team had the rare pleasure of making fresh footprints in the white world of the forest.

Only the animals had preceded them, for Per Garson's skis cut across the hills where feet and sleds could not follow. So the new snow showed only the stars of small animal paws and now and then a round spot where a rabbit may have sat on his haunches.

After a time Peter saw ski marks and noted that several pairs of snow shoes had traveled into the forest that morning.

He had an uneasy feeling. The ski trail was not Per Garson's for he would have come from an entirely different direction. Near the cave he picked up another trail that seemed to come in a great loop from behind the evergreens at the cave entrance. Then, farther on, the loop sent off a shoot the way a branch grows out of a tree.

Peter was cautious about approaching the cave. He was not going to walk into a trap. When he first came on the ski trail he warned his team to silence. So the ten of them moved over the snow as quietly as possible. Near the cave he lined his boys and girls behind a thick clump of bushes that the new snow had made into a solid blot of white. Leaving them to guard his sled he quietly followed the trail into the cave.

He would not have been surprised to see grey-green Nazi uniforms inside. But instead, there was only Per Garson wiping his forehead on his sleeve.

Peter's stealthy approach was not lost on old Per.

"So you was frightened, eh? You think to come on the Germans? I should have told you it was only us."

"There are snowshoe trails, too. Down the gully beyond the trolls' tree."

"Na, na. Not to worry about them. Miles and Ole made them. One hour more then there'll be trails all ways you can look, of snowshoes, of skis and of just plain feet. No one could find the way here by following the marks you boys and girls make with your boots and sleds."

"Well, I didn't know," Peter said. "I knew you had come across the valley but I didn't think one pair of skis could make so many trails. And I didn't know about the snowshoes."

"I make the many ski trails myself. I make more when you go off." Per drew out a blue bandanna handkerchief and wiped his running eyes. "You thought the Germans knew already about the cave? Not yet, but we must be careful or they'll learn."

"So you and Ole and Miles are making a lot of trails so they can't follow?" Peter had to admire the forethought behind this.

"And why not? Without them, what could be easier than to know everything? As plain as the noses on their faces would be the way. From all the houses come footprints and sled marks. They all go to one place, to the woods. So if you're a German what do you do? You follow the tracks and they lead you to a cave that is no cave at all, only what was put here by someone with something to hide. Well, what is there to hide? Nothing but these brown bricks. And what are these bricks for? They're not to build a wall. One doesn't wrap such bricks in brown covers. And they're not for the fire. It takes only a minute to slit open the covers. And what do you find? Why just plain gold, gold enough to pave a street!"

It was a long speech for Per Garson, longer than any Peter had ever heard from him. Nor was that all of it, either. "And if you think we're going to let the Germans have this gold just by following the footprints that go straight as arrows, you're mistaken, Master Peter."

What a vast amount of detail this undertaking required. Why the grownups thought of everything! Peter could not help being impressed with the precautions that were being taken to prevent discovery. He felt that his safety and that of all the children was being guarded to the utmost. He felt glad that he knew about this. But Per Garson did not allow him much time for reflection.

"Where's your sled?" he asked sharply.

Peter replied with a scurry through the door.

"It's all right, kids," he called. "Come on, and bring my sled."

*   *   *

The storm hadn't destroyed the German barracks. This the children could see when they reached the lookout.

Beaten by the wind and lashed by the sea, they still stood trim beside the fishing pier. One of the Nazi warehouses had suffered some damage for a crew of workers was busy repairing its roof. The big fiord had been on a rampage because there was wreckage along its shore. But whether it was German or Norse property that had been carried away, the children couldn't tell.

"The Nazis didn't know what to make of the storm," Helga decided when her team reached the point where the beach lay spread before her. Peter's team was already there. His boys and girls had lunched and were about to start down the mountain to the Snake. "They didn't know whether they'd be drowned like the people in the Flood in the Bible," she said. "They wouldn't have had time to build an ark."

In any event, being housebound for three days hadn't improved the Commandant's disposition. Peter could see that from where he was watching. The head officer was striding up and down before the barracks. Hands

behind his back, he would now and again lift a leather riding crop to shake it at someone who displeased him. Even up at the lookout they could hear the snarl of his voice.

"He's telling them they are stupid as Norwegians." Helga had studied a little German and was translating for her team. "He says that the people of this country have better sense than they for they build their houses for the crazy wild weather in this part of the world."

"He must think we have blizzards like this all the time," Peter cut in.

Helga went on. "He says that if he'd been there when the barracks were started, they wouldn't have had all this trouble."

"I guess the storm did them more damage than we know," Peter concluded as he gathered his team together for the final push to the Snake.

Down on the beach Peter had his first brush with the Commandant.

"Big boy like you, playing with a sled!" he taunted. "In Germany you'd be one of Hitler's Youth. You'd learn to march. You'd be on your way to being a soldier!"

"Don't want to learn to march. Don't want to be a soldier like you," Peter said under his breath.

"I could use a boy like you," the Commandant went on. "To polish my boots and bring me shaving water. What about it, boy? Would you like to come live here in the barracks?"

Peter, of course, made no reply. The Commandant strode over and stood directly above him. Seated on his sled he began to be afraid the officer would yank him up by his coat.

"Speak, boy. Are you dumb?"

But Peter had no word to say. He was too frightened to speak, even if it were not forbidden.

"Dumb stupid cattle, you Norwegians." The Commandant turned on his heel. "You deserve to lose your country. You're too brainless to defend it. But we'll put an end to this sled riding. There's no sense in a whole country growing up in ignorance. On Monday you go back to school."

CHAPTER SIXTEEN

PETER chuckled to himself.

The Commandant didn't know that Mr. Anders, the schoolmaster, had joined the Norwegian Army, had gone away to fight.

There would be no school, no matter what the Commandant ordered.

But that was reckoning without that resolute individual. There would be school if a German officer had to teach it, the grown folks had been told. When they first heard of the new order they sent a committee to tell the Commandant about Mr. Anders, and such was his reply.

When Peter came back from the Holms' farm the next day he saw German soldiers posting notices throughout the town. They had nailed long white handbills to the church door and on the post office and on the very school itself. Now they were putting additional ones on the light poles.

The handbills were printed in Norwegian. They said that all must go about their lives as before the German occupation. Fishing and canning must be commenced as soon as the weather permitted. The soil must be planted as fully as in former times. Above all, the notices told, the children must return to school.

"Nothing more quickly demoralizes a civilian population than to have its children idle," the notices proclaimed.

Peter watched the soldiers at work. Everything they did was neat and thorough. They brought their own tools, even to a short ladder. A corporal and a squad of eight marched to a corner, saluted stiffly and divided into groups. Thus they went about their tasks, informing the people of Riswyk the will of the German force of occupation.

One of the soldiers was the blue-eyed private Peter had noticed the first day the Germans had come to Norway. He looked wistful then, and today seemed sadder than ever. It was as if he hated sending the children back to their books.

"Hello," he said shyly in Peter's own language. But, of course, Peter could not reply. And seeing him close, Peter thought he looked younger than the others. He would be twenty or twenty-one at the most, Peter fancied.

To the children the German uniform was a common enough sight. But among the grown folks it caused consternation. In truth, the Germans had stayed by themselves on the beach near their barracks and only in rare instances had come up the mountain to the town.

But if their appearance caused a commotion among the townspeople of Riswyk, they did not show it. They chose to act as if they did not know the Germans were there. The German soldiers stared frankly, but the Norwegians walked along the streets with their heads in the air. They finished their errands hurriedly and went to their homes and stayed there. Then the minute the soldiers marched out of town they began coming out of their houses.

They gathered around the notices to study the new orders. There was a little procession to the pastry shop, the *konditeri*. Peter saw his mother coming out of their house. He stacked his sled against the wall and ran to join her.

"The notice, Mother. You've read it? It says school must open on Monday."

"Yes, I know." Mrs. Lundstrom quickened her steps.

Inside the *konditeri*, a little knot of people had already gathered. They had come not so much to order the inviting looking sandwiches nor the delicious little iced cakes and pie crust goodies as to discuss this latest order. But there was no need for anyone to say aloud the question that was first in their thoughts.

With school reopened, how are we going to get the gold to the Snake?

Mrs. Lundstrom felt they should be careful about discussing it and warned the others to caution. The soldiers had barely left the town. They might return.

"I'll take a dozen of your raisin cookies, Fru Flack," she said. "*And do be careful,*" she was saying when the door actually did open and in came a Nazi recruit, "that you wrap them carefully," she finished lamely.

The soldier was the blue-eyed private who had said "hello" to Peter. He only wanted a *smorsbord*. He chose one of the open egg and herring sandwiches and asked for a cup of coffee. Then he took a seat at one of the tables by the wall, his back to the women at the counter. Fru Flack brought him his order.

He began to eat his *smorsbord* slowly at first and then more rapidly. With his entrance, the many busy tongues were stilled. Not a single syllable had been spoken the entire time he was there. When his own words died away there was a complete silence. As if he realized that all eyes were on his back, he ate his sandwich and tried to drink the steaming coffee. But it was too hot. After a couple of mouthfuls he pushed aside the cup, rose and took his leave.

"You see?" Mrs. Lundstrom stretched out her hands. "I don't want to spoil your day's sales, Fru Flack, but I think it would be better if we talked about this in our homes."

Peter picked up the box of pastries his mother had bought and followed her out of the door. But she did not go home as she had advised the others to do. She walked along the diagonal of the town square to its opposite side and beyond to the home of Dr. Aker.

She lifted the brass knocker. Marta, the housekeeper, smiled in welcome. Yes, the doctor was home. Would Fru Lundstrom and Peter come in?

They entered the doctor's study, cheerful with its chintz-covered furniture and shining hearth brasses. Dr. Aker gave them a cordial welcome.

"Come, sit down." His good face shone only a little less brightly than the andirons. "I'll have Marta brew you a cup of tea."

Mrs. Lundstrom dropped into a deep chair the doctor drew up for her. Peter sat down beside her on a stool.

"And how are you, Doctor?" she asked as he fussed with the fire.

"Never better, Fru Lundstrom. I think the blizzard did a lot of good to my old bones. I tell you I feel spry."

"That's just what happened to Per Garson," Mrs. Lundstrom said. "He complained constantly before the storm. Now he never mentions any pains."

"Well, we old people have a way of feeling things that you young ones know nothing about. It's sort of an added sense."

"Is there any sickness in the town, Doctor?" Mrs. Lundstrom asked.

"I must say, Fru Lundstrom, Riswyk has never had a healthier winter. I think the long cold is beneficial. It seems to have killed the germs."

"But I saw you going out during the blizzard. I thought someone must be very sick to get you out on such a day."

"It was only to see Granny Gohla. The poor soul gets pretty lonesome living by herself. She's always so glad for company. So I make it a point of seeing her twice a week. It was my day to go and I didn't want to disappoint her."

Peter's mother returned to the subject of illnesses but the doctor disclaimed any for the town. "I tell you, Fru Lundstrom, a doctor has a hard time getting along in Riswyk. A healthier community you won't find anywhere on earth."

The housekeeper brought in the tea tray and Mrs. Lundstrom filled the role of hostess in pouring out. There was buttered toast and strawberry jam, Peter saw with pleasure.

"You've been out today, Doctor? You read the notice?"

"Yes, I read it when I went for my walk. A good

thing, too, I thought. It's best to keep the people busy, especially the children."

"But, Doctor Aker, going back to school will stop—" Peter began.

"Peter!" his mother silenced him. But there was something in Dr. Aker's face that told them he understood what Peter started to say.

"I'd quite forgotten about that," he said. "I'd forgotten what reopening the school will mean. After school is too late, I suppose."

Mrs. Lundstrom stirred her tea. The wood cracked in the fireplace.

"Wait a minute, Fru Lundstrom," the doctor set his cup precisely on the tea tray. "You were asking about the sick. Now I'm not sure I told you the whole truth. You see, we doctors don't like to alarm the townsfolk but in the winter one can always expect some sickness."

"And widespread sickness amounts to an epidemic," Mrs. Lundstrom added.

"And during an epidemic one always closes the school," Dr. Aker finished.

An epidemic! Yes, if they had to make one.

CHAPTER SEVENTEEN

A NEW disease found its way into Riswyk.

It attacked only the smallest children, the ones who had not yet started to school.

They were covered with red spots from head to foot.

But the disease differed from the better-known rashes like diphtheria and scarlet fever. The patient had no high temperature. His appetite could be just as good as before the rash. Indeed, Dr. Aker did not insist that the children stop eating. He only said they must stay indoors while covered with the red spots.

"What is this new disease?" the people asked each other. Dr. Aker told them a name of many syllables. They could never remember it so they called it the plague.

"German measles" was Peter's name for it and with reason. He had been in Dr. Aker's study when he packed his bag before going to visit Bunny, the first of his patients. Peter had seen him put in a bottle of red disinfectant that he used for cuts and bruises. Cotton on the end of a toothpick made a good paint brush. Bunny Lundstrom had as thick a coat of spots as the leopard of his Noah's Ark.

Bunny was told he was quarantined. He had no idea what that meant until his mother explained that Peter and Lovisa would go live at Helga Thomsen's house while Bunny had those spots. So quarantined meant that

Peter and Lovisa had to go away from home, he decided.

The three-year-old Dal twins were sick, too. And Ole's two-year-old son, Little Ole. But as none of these had big brothers or sisters, Peter and Lovisa had the distinction of being the only ones turned out of their homes while the disease raged.

School? Well school was out of the question during an epidemic. Dr. Aker went to the Commandant to explain why his order could not be carried out. Some of the children, he told, were dangerously ill. It might be fatal for the whole town, for the Germans themselves, if the disease was not checked at once. To open the school would be a sure way to spread it.

On his return from the beach, Dr. Aker found Mrs. Lundstrom and Peter waiting in his office for news of his interview with the Commandant and of how the doctor found himself trapped by making his plague so unusual.

"'How long will this disease last?' the Commandant asked me. But I could not tell. 'It's a new thing with us,' I said, 'a disease I've never treated before. It could run nine days like measles or thirty days like scarlet fever. But we're taking every precaution. We're isolating and disinfecting.'"

"When I said it could spread to the troops on the beach I thought he looked white. He sent for the German army doctor, a civil enough fellow named Metzger. This Metzger began asking me a long list of questions. Were the tongues coated? Was there undue perspiration? Was there a high fever? He seemed surprised with my answers and none too well satisfied. Then he nearly had me when he proposed something I hadn't thought about at all."

" 'I'll take a look at one of your cases, Doctor. I'll go back with you when you go,' he said to me."

"Well, he had me there," Dr. Aker went on. "It was the last thing I expected. It hadn't occurred to me that an army doctor would be called in for civilian illness, and if so, that he would insist on seeing for himself. One look by him and the epidemic would be over. Those spots might deceive an ordinary person but they'd never fool a doctor."

"Yes, and that would arouse suspicion," Mrs. Lundstrom said. "Maybe they don't suspect us of anything yet. But if they learn we have a reason for keeping the school closed, they'll begin to ask what it is and possibly find out."

Peter was open-eyed as the doctor went on with his story.

"Well, I had to think fast," he said. "I couldn't behave as if I didn't want him for that would surely make them inquire why he couldn't see one of the patients. So I said, 'There's nothing I would like better, Doctor. I'm distressed at how quickly this sickness spreads. I'd appreciate another opinion. For it seems to travel like wildfire. I'm not sure but what it could spread to your whole camp here.' "

"I thought the Commandant drew away from me when I started to tell of the disease. He acted as if I could give it to him just by being there. But now I saw him sort of jump. But Dr. Metzger didn't seem afraid.

'If it's as fast a thing as that, I would indeed like to see one of your cases,' he said."

"The Commandant, however, had a different idea. My words about how it might travel to the whole camp had struck home. He made a sign to the doctor. They went into a little room nearby. I could hear only a buzz of talk and now and again some words I could understand. Dr. Metzger was trying to win his permission to visit Riswyk and see the new rash for himself but the other was firm."

"'Our men were up there, yesterday,' I overheard the Commandant say. 'You'll have all you can do to see they don't come down with this disease.' He said some other things I didn't hear but I caught some words to the effect that they were living in a heathenish outlandish place where a blizzard could blow up out of a calm,

and that the diseases were probably as freakish and un-expected as the weather. The best course for them to follow was to have as little as possible to do with the people. When they came back to me, the doctor spoke."

" 'It will not be necessary for me to see any of your patients,' he said. 'Continue with the treatment you've begun and keep a careful quarantine.' Then he gave me a long list of orders about sanitation, and burning waste and so on. When he finished, the Commandant said, 'Remember, if this disease spreads to our army, you'll be held accountable.' "

"I could give him my word that none of his soldiers would take the disease."

Mrs. Lundstrom and Peter had to laugh. Nothing but the red disinfectant and the cotton-tipped toothpicks could spread Bunny's strange disease.

"He waved his hand at me to tell me I was dismissed," Dr. Aker went on. " 'I've taken the liberty of closing the school,' I told him. 'I've also ordered all healthy children to stay outdoors whenever possible. There's nothing like fresh air to check an epidemic,' I said."

So the children's task could go on in spite of all that had happened to prevent it.

Bunny recovered and Lovisa and Peter were allowed to go back to their home. So it was a short-lived disease, the townsfolk decided. Like three-day measles. But there were enough new cases to keep the school closed.

•　　•　　•

So the gold kept spilling down the mountain, thousands and thousands of kroners of bullion every day.

Two teams would go out one morning and two teams the following day. On every sled was more gold than any of the children had ever seen before.

One day Helga's team got the start on Peter's. When he reached the Snake her team was already there. She seemed buried in her own thoughts. When Peter approached she hardly answered his wave of greeting.

When he began unloading his sled she came over beside him and dropped on her knees in the snow. "Peter," she whispered, "I'm frightened. I heard something."

"Heard something? What?"

"Listen," she warned, still in whispers. "There it is again. It's even louder here than over by my snowman."

"I don't hear anything."

"Look! Something moved in the bushes!" She pointed to the far side of the fiord.

They ran in the direction she pointed. They pushed through the snow-hung brush but were stopped by the black water at their feet. They were unable to cross the angry rushing stream to the far side where the snow made a thick screen over the heavier shrubbery.

"If we could only get over, we could see the prints in the snow."

"Are we being watched?" Peter asked.

"I don't know. For the last week I've felt eyes on me every time I've turned around."

CHAPTER EIGHTEEN

UNCLE VICTOR would have to be warned if someone were spying at the Snake. But Peter had no way of finding him. If his boat were hidden by camouflage as Herr Holm suggested, covered by trees and snow to make it hard to see, it might also be concealed by one of the bends of the twisted stream.

Peter had had no sight of the *Cleng Peerson* since he had been aboard her in the autumn. For weeks now he had strained his eyes and searched both banks of the fiord, but all he had seen was the black water and white snow.

It would be useless to search for the *Cleng* he knew. Besides, it would be downright dangerous. If they were being watched it would give the whole thing away. To add a boat to the buried gold was as simple as adding two and two. No one could fail to know what they were doing.

So all he could do was to get back to Riswyk and tell his mother or Per Garson. Maybe they knew some way to get in touch with Uncle Victor.

Helga's team started up the mountain. Peter finished his snowman and waited for his small fry to finish theirs. He lent a hand where he could and soon there stood an army of soldiers, all in white fur coats like a ski patrol.

From the other side of the Snake, Peter could have climbed a woods trail that saved many miles on the road. But he had no way to cross. Nor could he leave his team. It was up to him to see that they were all brought back to Riswyk the following day. He was responsible that none of them said a single word to the Germans.

Helga's warning kept coming back, "For this last week I've felt eyes on me every time I've turned around."

For some time now, he'd had an uneasy feeling himself. Only he wasn't going to admit it. But when Helga spoke right out like that—well, what could you do? It fairly gave you the shivers.

For one thing there was always the thought that things were going too well. For four weeks now, they'd been taking gold down the mountains under the very noses of the Germans. Except for trying to reopen the school the Germans had made no attempt to stop them. Perhaps they knew all along what they were doing. Perhaps they were letting them have all the hard work of hauling thirteen tons of gold down the mountain only to find they were aiding the invaders. They were being left alone to do the work and the Germans would step in and take the gold.

If only he could talk to Uncle Victor! If only he knew that the bricks were taken aboard the *Cleng Peerson* every night! But they must be. For every time he returned to the Snake the snow soldiers were lying on the ground.

"Come on, everyone." Peter was impatient at his lagging team. "We'll be caught if we don't hurry."

The Germans had issued a new order, a curfew. None could be out after sunset.

The long shadows of late afternoon made blue streaks on the woody sides of the mountain as the children dragged their sleds up its slope. Both borders of the road were heavily timbered but there were stretches where the brush was less thick and these were crisscrossed with ski trails. Following the blizzard, the Germans had adopted the custom of the country. They had taken to skiing. Some were clumsy and the children, who could ski almost as soon as they could walk, roared with laughter at their struggles. There was one fat lieutenant who spent most of his time on the seat of his pants, they said. He would start down the merest side of a hill to find himself sitting in the snow, his feet straight out before him.

"Lieutenant Sit-Down," they called him to themselves.

But not all the Germans were as awkward as the big officer. A few could do a Christiania turn as gracefully as any Norwegian, though this was hotly debated by children and grownups.

"Of course some of them can ski," Peter had to admit. "How do you think they got into our country?" he asked Lovisa. "A lot of them came weeks ago by train in disguise. They brought their skis and pretended they'd come for the winter sports. Then they learned all about us and our defenses. They showed the way to the ones who came by parachutes and those who pretended to be sailors on the freight boats."

Tonight, they would have to run for it to be at the Holms' farm before sunset. Peter increased his pace and urged his team to hasten theirs.

They were passing the place where Peter would have come out on the road if he could have crossed the fiord and taken the short-cut up the rocks. The trail went straight up for a time. When it reached a crest it dipped down again to meet the road below.

The wind had blown the dry snow off the branches of some of the pines. They looked black against the white of the forest.

Out of the dark pines just ahead shot a German soldier on skis.

CHAPTER NINETEEN

S
O THAT was what Helga heard and saw at the Snake—this Nazi soldier!

There could be no mistake. The trail he had taken could have come only from the Snake.

From where he was Peter could not see the soldier's face. But the cut of his uniform was unmistakable and against its grey were the markings of his service corps.

So they'd been spied on after all. Peter forgot to be afraid. He was only angry—angry and sorry.

To think that all their hard work had been for nothing. Just now he was so tired he could hardly make his feet move ahead. And what was he tired for, this night and every night? For the Germans who came in and took their country and said what they must do and not do and what time they must be in their houses at night.

Well, Peter resolved, they weren't going to have the gold, not if there was still a chance to save it.

Uncle Victor would certainly have to be warned. But how? To find him at night would be impossible when Peter couldn't even find him in the daytime. He could leave his team in the Holms' care that night. But to go back to the Snake to look for his uncle was out of the question. There was the curfew, for one thing. And Peter was so tired he could have lain right down in the snow and slept.

Perhaps Herr Holm could help him. Maybe he could

find Uncle Victor's boat. Or he could hitch up his sleigh and go to Riswyk and ask Peter's mother or Per Garson. But would he dare risk disobeying the curfew? He could get shot if he were caught. It said so on the notice on the school door.

The Holms had serious faces when Peter told of seeing the Nazi soldier on skis.

"We're all in on this," Herr Holm said. "If we're being trapped, I'm the first to face the firing squad. Night after night I harbor you children."

But Peter thought he didn't seem much afraid.

"Your mother'll certainly have to be told," he decided. "The teams of Lovisa and Michael will be starting out in the morning. We cannot let them be caught and the gold taken."

"We could head them off when they pass here," Fru Holm suggested.

"But where could we hide the gold? It wouldn't be safe here and there's no use having them haul it all that distance just to cart it back. No, I'll have to talk it over with Fru Lundstrom. I'll go tonight."

"Tonight? But you can't. There's the curfew." His wife spoke sharply.

"I must. There's no other way. Fru Lundstrom'll know what to do."

"But you could be shot."

"They'll have to catch me first. A sheet for me, Mama, and off I go."

Over his heavy outdoor clothes he draped a sheet. It fell in folds from his shoulders to his feet.

"Now a towel for the head." This he twisted into a turban. "Now do you think they'll know me from the snow?"

They went outside with him while he strapped on his skis. "Lucky they're down on the beach, not up here. If I'm fortunate I won't meet any Germans."

"They could be in the woods, Papa." The good farm-wife was anxious.

"Then I'll hide." He took up his ski poles. "Well, I'm off to tell your mother about this spy," he addressed Peter. "She'll surely know some way to get in touch with your uncle."

The next morning when Peter awoke he was alone in the barn. The others had gone long before, Fru Holm told him.

"We called them and sent them back to Riswyk as always. That far they could go without a leader."

"But why was I allowed to sleep?" Peter wanted to know.

"Papa brought word from your mother you're to stay here until she comes. We did not call you because you seemed so tired and she won't be here till afternoon."

"Then Herr Holm got through all right?"

"They'd have to be smart to catch that slippery Norseman," she boasted. "He was at your mother's and back before midnight."

Peter sighed in relief. So the Germans and their old curfew didn't mean much, after all. But if he'd been caught—Peter shuddered. The penalty was posted on the school door.

"Why am I to wait for Mother?" he asked.

"She's going to look for your Uncle Victor. You're to go along in case we need to get in touch with him again. Papa and your mama and Per Garson thought it best for you to go."

So he would have to go back to the Snake that very day and maybe face the Commandant who wanted to make him his servant. Well, it didn't matter. Herr Holm was safe and Uncle Victor would be warned. That was all that counted.

It was one o'clock when a bobsled turned into the farmyard. Pulling it was Peter's mother and on it sat Bunny and two other small children. Bunny smiled all over to see his brother in this strange place.

"Peter," his mother greeted him, "I'm glad you had a nice long rest."

"But how are you going to find Uncle Victor?" he asked.

"I have a chart of the Snake right here," she tapped her pocket. "The *Cleng Peerson*'s marked with a cross. Uncle Victor left it in case we needed to know."

"You'll have to walk when you reach the beach," Peter warned. "I don't know if these little fellows can walk all that distance."

"Then I'll pull them. I meant to, anyway. For the looks of it, Peter. Tomorrow and the next day Mrs. Berg and Mrs. Olsen and some of the others are going to go down and take the babies."

Peter understood. Anything to throw the Germans off the scent. For unless the spies already knew everything, no one would look for anything out of order from a woman with a sled load of children.

"We can carry a little gold, too," his mother said. "Every bit counts and this snow isn't going to last forever."

CHAPTER TWENTY

PETER transferred the gold from the bobsled to his own sled. He gave his mother a start for he knew he could overtake her whenever he wished.

Mrs. Lundstrom sat on the bobsled and steered it skilfully. But with the children on it, she didn't dare take the long stretches with the speed Peter could have made.

Down on the beach he was angry to find his mother the object of much curiosity.

Soldiers were filing into the open space before the barracks. Their drill master made them stand at attention while she pulled the long sled past their lines. The drill master froze in stiff salute.

"Thank the merciful heavens he had not said 'Heil Hitler,'" Peter breathed in relief. For she would have had to make some reply, and Peter knew his mother was not the one to praise a man who had brought evil to her country. And yet, she would have had to say something. If she had refused—well anything could have happened. People were sent to concentration camps for as little a thing as that, for failing to exalt the German leader.

Peter wanted to tie his sled to the long one to help his mother pull the children over the level stretch but she told him to go ahead.

"It's the looks of the thing, Peter," she whispered.

He was glad he had gone on when, a minute later, he

heard the voice of the Commandant. Peter knew he was addressing his mother but he dared not turn around to look. He'd been lucky to escape as lightly as he had, the day the officer stopped him and asked if he would like to be his servant.

"Good morning, good lady. You've a fine day for your sled ride." Peter knew his precise Norwegian accent.

His mother made no answer.

"If you like, I'll have one of my men pull that sled," he spoke politely.

Still his mother was silent. Then from up the beach Peter could see Lieutenant Sit-Down coming toward him and toward the Commandant. He had a paper in his hand. He paid no attention to Peter but went rapidly toward the chief officer. Peter could just make out the click of his heels as he bowed in salute. He must have handed the paper to the Commandant for there was silence as if the latter were reading a message. Then the Commandant addressed the lieutenant in German. Peter knew only a little German but he had no difficulty making out what was said.

"These Norwegians! Have they no manners? They're so many boors. Or is it ears they lack? There was a boy here one day. I offered to let him help my orderlies. He acted as if he couldn't hear."

Peter dug into the snow as hard as he could. He was that boy. He was afraid the Commandant might recognize his back.

He reached the cliff that hid the Snake. From there he watched his mother pulling hard on the rope of the bobsled. It seemed to him that she would never arrive at the wall that would hide her from the eyes of those hundreds of Germans.

Slowly she traveled over the snow. She had to turn into the valley before Peter dared give her a hand on the rope.

"But the snow soldiers are all knocked down," she noted. "That means that Victor and Rolls came out last night and loaded the gold you children brought yesterday. Could you and Helga possibly be mistaken?"

"Helga's nearly always right," Peter spoke ruefully. It was a sore point. Helga had been right and he wrong in so many disputes. "If Helga says she's seen anything, you can be pretty sure she has."

Mrs. Lundstrom had to agree. Helga was known as "bright" throughout Riswyk.

"Anyway, I saw a soldier on skis just before we turned into Holms' farm last night. He would have had to come from here. There's nowhere else he could have come from."

"In any event we'll have to tell Uncle Victor so he can be on guard. Now the thing to do is to find the boat." Mrs. Lundstrom drew from her pocket a drawing of the Snake with the *Cleng Peerson* marked with a cross.

"But that's right here," she said. "Here are the two fallen trees."

"There's no boat here," Peter announced triumphantly. "I looked for it every day and I've not seen it yet."

"I think the children will be safe while we look," his mother said. "Bunny, you and Dag and Ingrid make a snow castle, a great big one. Look, I'll help you start it."

She dropped on the snow beside them. Peter stood the bobsled on its end. It would screen them, a little, from the wind. Then he untied the bricks he had transferred from his mother's sled to his own. These he buried in a drift. In no time at all a snow man was standing guard over them.

And now for the *Cleng Peerson.*

But although it was clearly marked on the drawing, there was nothing of it to be seen. Not a spar, not a boom, not a foot of the mast. Only the everlasting snow, the pines and the jutting cliffs that made pincers around the black rushing stream and its narrow borders of land.

Peter and his mother walked to the very edge of the water. In the little wooded strip they saw a strange new kind of vegetation. The forest seemed to dance. Pines they thought rooted in the bank, now seemed to have no roots at all but were bobbing up and down with the rush of the current.

And now that they were in a part of the valley where something was amiss, they could see other strange sights. Through the thick brush on the bank they could just about make out the *Cleng Peerson.* But what a strange *Cleng Peerson.* Pines were growing right out of her hull. Her mast was a towering evergreen. The branches thickened at the crow's nest and then tapered to a stately point.

"A pretty good job of camouflage, don't you think?" a voice spoke softly at their side. Both of them jumped in fright.

CHAPTER TWENTY-ONE

IT WAS Uncle Victor who had spoken. It took some minutes for Mrs. Lundstrom and Peter to recover from their astonishment. When they did they realized that they were being shown up a fir-screened gangplank. At its head stood Rolls, the mate, with a hand to help them alight on the dancing deck.

"But you're not the ones to be surprised," Victor was saying. "What about me? I was expecting the two teams as usual. Instead I find only you two and Bunny and his friends."

The *Cleng Peerson* was a fishing smack of fifty tons. She had been built long before Uncle Victor's time for the herring industry. She carried a sloop rig and could set a course and square sail. But Uncle Victor had installed a thirteen-horsepower engine. So the *Cleng* had no need to wait for a wind but could travel under her own force at all times.

When newer and finer boats were built in the shipyards of the coast, people would ask Victor Lundstrom why he didn't get one.

"Why do you sail that tub?" they would question, knowing he could afford the finest.

To people who spoke in such fashion, Uncle Victor had little to say. But Peter knew what his uncle thought about the *Cleng*.

"There never was such a ship in the whole history of navigation," he once told Peter. "She's the sturdiest thing afloat. And she's as easy to manage as a kitten. As for capacity, well, for her size, she's the beat of anything you ever heard tell of. Why I could carry food and fuel for five years if I ever decided to make a Polar expedition!"

When Uncle Victor bought the smack years ago, he changed her name. There were those who asked why the name *Cleng Peerson*. But Peter knew why his uncle called the boat he loved after one of his heroes. Cleng Peerson was the Norseman who went to America and who, because of his bravery in the face of hardships, was called the Norwegian Daniel Boone.

"I'll give you tea, although I didn't expect visitors," Uncle Victor showed them into his cabin.

One of the greatest thrills of Peter's childhood was to have tea aboard the *Cleng*. But alas, invitations were hard to get. Uncle Victor was a busy man with his fishing crews and the *Cleng* was at sea much of the time.

It was all so cheery and bright aboard the ship. In the cabin Peter could see his face reflected in a dozen different surfaces. It was spotless as only a ship's cabin can be. Leather bunks along two sides served as seats in the daytime. Over one of these were two port holes, darkened now by the camouflage shrubbery outside. But there were peep holes in the shrubbery and through them came a jagged broken light. A large round table centered the cabin. It was fastened to the deck and above it hung a lamp on a chain. About the only other thing of importance was a large map of Europe as it was in the nineteen thirties. The map was draped with the red field and white-bordered blue cross of the flag of Norway.

"And what is the news of Lars?" Victor asked about his brother.

"There's little to tell," Mrs. Lundstrom said sadly. "His regiment got to Trondheim and that's about all we know."

"There's been fierce fighting there." Uncle Victor lit a spirit lamp. He told what he had been able to learn about the army. His visitors listened eagerly. Then Mrs. Lundstrom explained the purpose of their visit.

"We didn't come to make a social call," she said. "I don't dare leave Bunny and the others very long. They may get tired and wander away. We came to warn you that someone may be watching you. Helga Thomsen said she heard something and saw someone move down here yesterday. Then Peter saw a German soldier on skis come out of the trail from here that cuts the road near Holms'."

Uncle Victor looked grave. "It could have been Rolls or me that Helga saw. We've been watching every move these youngsters make. They haven't come once that one or the other of us hasn't stood guard."

"Yes, we thought as much," Mrs. Lundstrom said. "We talked of that last night when Herr Holm brought the news. I wouldn't have given it a thought if Peter hadn't seen the soldier on skis come out of the trail."

Uncle Victor had set the kettle on a spirit lamp and now lifted the lid to see if it was boiling.

"You could tell from the snow prints," Peter suggested.

"Yes, we could. After a distance. But it's pretty well trampled around here with Rolls and me going out night after night to bring the gold aboard. But one of us will go up the trail tonight and see," his uncle answered.

"But the curfew?"

Uncle Victor only laughed. He made the tea and poured it and passed the cups to his guests. There were spice cakes that Rolls brought in from the galley.

"There's no such thing as being too cautious about spies," Uncle Victor said after a time. "But if anyone had been here in the daylight, surely Rolls or I would have seen him. Of course I did take forty winks yesterday afternoon when the children were here. You see, when the two of us dig up and carry on board almost a thousand pounds of gold, it's pretty late and we're tired. We've things to do in the morning to get ready to sail. So we have to catch up on our sleep when we can. But Rolls was around, weren't you, old fellow?"

"Yes, I was. But when I saw Peter I knew everything'd be all right. I'd left my pipe on board and I came back just long enough to smoke a pipeful."

"Then someone could have been around and neither you nor I would have known."

"Is there much more gold to load?" Victor asked his sister-in-law after a pause.

"No. You have nearly all of it. Per Garson's been checking. The last of next week will finish it. And it won't be six weeks until Tuesday. We've been lucky, Victor. Think, if the thaws had come earlier."

"Well, you can't get it down here too soon to suit me."

He stirred his tea. "This business of hanging around isn't exactly safe."

"You mean you're ready to sail?" Peter asked. "As soon as the gold's loaded you can go to America?"

"That's right, son. That's exactly what I mean."

"Then you know where the mines are laid?"

"Sure, I've known that for weeks, since we entered the war on the side of Britain and France. So hurry and get the gold down here so I can be under way. It'll be bad enough for the rest of you if we're caught, but Rolls and I would be shot."

"Oh, Uncle Victor!"

"But don't worry. We're not going to get caught. It's too much money to give the Germans and, anyway, I'd like to see New York again."

CHAPTER TWENTY-TWO

U NCLE VICTOR wasn't going to get shot if Peter could help it. He resolved then and there to do all he could to hurry the rest of the gold to the Snake so the *Cleng* could lift anchor and get away.

"There's nothing to do but what we've been doing," Victor Lundstrom decided. "We'll have to chance that this spy, or whatever he is, is still mystified and wants to learn more about us before he tells on us. He probably doesn't know that the bricks are gold bars because not one of them has been touched. Every sled load has been accounted for. So the best we can do is to get the rest of it here and let me get away while there's still a chance."

They agreed they had no choice in the matter.

"Yes, we've started it," Mrs. Lundstrom said. "The only thing to do now is to finish it."

The visitors dared stay no longer aboard the *Cleng* because of the little children.

"This is good-by, Victor." Mrs. Lundstrom kissed her brother-in-law. "God bless and keep you always. You've undertaken a mighty task. Only a man as brave as you would attempt it."

Uncle Victor disclaimed the heroism.

"Not at all," he said. "I'm the lucky one. I'm going to get out of this while the rest of you have to stay and face it. Rolls and I have it easy. It's Lars and the ones who have gone to fight who are the brave ones."

Again Peter had to precede his mother along the beach past the German camp. He waited for her up on the road beyond the bend where he could not be seen from below. When at length she reached him, he tied his sled to the end of the bobsled and together they pulled up the steep hillside.

At the Holm farm there was a flurry of excitement. That much was evident the minute they turned in from the road. Fru Holm wanted to tell them something. But she was silent until the small children had eaten their bread and milk and were tucked into bed.

"There's something strange going on," she waved a wooden cooking spoon. "But first—" She went to the door and looked out. Then she bolted it and came over to where they sat beside the fire.

"Today, just before you came, I saw a German soldier in my woods. He was wearing skis. But why would he be skiing about my place? I ask myself. He comes cautiously as if he's looking for something. I watch and he comes close to my barn. Then he slides himself along with his poles and pulls himself up the runway into my barn. INTO MY BARN, I tell you!"

Peter and his mother had no word to say about this new menace. Was the German spying around the Holms' farm because he knew the boys were put to sleep there? Peter wondered. Fru Holm went on.

"I think I will call out to him, 'Get out of my barn, you loafer.' But then I think, No, that's bad. It might make him angry and he would turn me over to the officers. So I say to myself, I'll say nothing till I've talked with Fru Lundstrom."

"Then what happened?" Mrs. Lundstrom asked.

"I just waited and waited. By and by he came out and started back the way he'd come."

"Perhaps he's on a mission to get food for the soldiers," Mrs. Lundstrom suggested.

"Then why doesn't he come right up here and ask me or Papa?" she answered with spirit. "He needn't go around looking in people's barns."

None of them knew what to make of Fru Holm's visitor. Peter tried to find out what the soldier on skis looked like. He was anxious to know if he was the same soldier he had seen himself the day before. But he remembered he had seen nothing of that one but his back. So he could hardly compare the two.

Whatever the ski soldier was doing in Holms' barn, it could only mean danger for Uncle Victor. Peter determined they would make even greater haste getting the rest of the gold to the Snake. He and Michael and the bigger ones would have to take heavier loads, five bricks instead of four.

Then if the women were going to pull the long sleds, they could take some, too.

Things were happening too fast.

Well, he could always warn Uncle Victor. There was some comfort in knowing where to find the *Cleng*.

The next day, and for some days after that, Mrs. Berg and a number of the other women joined the children in their trips. They would take the bobsled and on each was a small pile of gold and over the gold sat the smallest children.

The next week the pile of bricks in the cave was

nearly down to the ground. There were less than a hundred to be sledded to the Snake. The children danced around in great glee.

"The snow's holding and we've done it!"

"We've done it! We've done it!" Helga was the noisiest.

"Shhh," Per Garson warned. "You've not done it yet. There's still nearly fifty sled loads. You can't say you've done it till this cave is bare as a miser's cupboard."

Nothing further was seen of the German soldier on skis. Peter was always on the watch. But not once did he see the grey-green uniform.

Late one afternoon he was unloading his sled in the Snake. He untied his rope and removed the sack covering and placed the bricks in the hole he had made in the snow.

He took two handfuls of snow and began to make his soldier. He patted it hard. As he reached for more, something made him look up. It was just the merest noise—soft like breathing.

He looked into a pair of blue, blue eyes. Their owner was wearing the dull-colored uniform of a German infantry soldier.

CHAPTER TWENTY-THREE

S O IT was all over.
They'd been discovered.

The Nazis knew what they were doing and had come to stop them.

Peter knelt in the snow, trembling. The blue eyes under the fringe of fair hair were familiar. Even in his fright Peter knew he had seen this private before. He'd seen him the very first day they'd passed the Nazi sentries. He had been helping unload the supplies. He was the one who had seemed to want to go sled riding too. More. He was the soldier who came to the *konditeri* for the *smorsbord*.

Then Peter had another surprise. The brush behind the soldier parted and Uncle Victor sprang out. He grabbed the soldier's arm and pinned them behind him and before he could make an outcry he had a gag over his mouth.

Behind Uncle Victor came Rolls, the mate. His revolver was pointed at the captive. When the latter made no effort to free himself, it was lowered. Then the men turned back into the brush towards the *Cleng Peerson*.

It all happened so fast that none but Peter saw. Not even Helga, a few feet away, knew what took place. She was hard at work on her snowman.

"Helga, take my team back with yours," Peter asked. "I want to see Uncle Victor."

Helga wanted to see Uncle Victor, too, and to go

aboard the *Cleng,* now that Peter knew where to find it. But Peter was president of the Defense Club. All of them had to obey him. When he refused to let her come with him, she had to do as he asked.

Peter had no idea whether or not his uncle would allow him aboard the boat. But he was going to find out. What was happening on the smack was something no boy of twelve was going to miss if he could help it. So he hurried through the brush to the side of the water.

From below the deck came strange sounds. Not to lose any of the excitement, Peter almost fell down the companionway in his haste.

Uncle Victor and Rolls had untied the prisoner's arms and had taken the gag from his mouth.

Then the captive soldier drew off his round army cap and threw it on the floor and tramped on it. He beat it with his feet, up and down. Then he tore at the insignia on his collar and tried to rip it off. All the while he was making hideous faces.

"What is it, man? Speak. Your mouth is no longer tied," Uncle Victor commanded sharply.

Then came a torrent of words, Norwegian and some other tongue Peter did not recognize.

"I'm no German even if I do wear the uniform. I'm a Pole. They took me and made me serve them, and the deceit is theirs, not mine."

"But what are you doing with a German army of occupation?" Uncle Victor asked.

"I tell you it is not my fault. It's theirs. I'm no more to blame than, than—than that boy there."

He pointed at Peter and now Uncle Victor and Rolls

saw him, too. But Uncle Victor made no move toward Peter. He gave him a glance that seemed to say, "It's all right. At your age I wouldn't have missed it, either."

"I want to go to the United States," the Pole went on. "If you'll take me on this boat, I'll cook and I'll scrub the decks. I'll sew the sails and carpenter. I'll stand watch. I'll do anything you ask. Only don't leave me here with those merciless machines, those Germans."

"What's he talking like that for?" Uncle Victor turned to Rolls. "What makes him think I'd take a man in a German uniform anywhere? How do I know he's a Pole and hates the Germans? Does he think I'm a baby to take him on his own word?"

Then he turned on the Pole and spoke severely.

"Come, now tell us what you know? How long have you been following these children?"

"If I follow the children, it's only because I'm lonely. It's because I want to be with someone I can like and trust. I will not make friends with the Germans. They don't even speak to me unless I can do them a service." Tears came into his blue eyes.

"Come, now, that's absurd. You have been following these children because you are spying on them. You want to find out what brings them here on their sleds. Then you go tell the Commandant and win a promotion. I know your sly German tricks."

"No. No. No. I have no sly German tricks. I'm a Pole. I have no love for the Germans. To me, they have done every wrong short of putting me to death. If I follow the children, it's not to do them harm."

He spoke convincingly. Peter believed he told the

truth. Even Uncle Victor seemed inclined to believe him for his next question was put in milder tones.

"But if you wanted to be with the children, why did you not make yourself known when you were here last week?"

"I was on the other side of the fiord. I could not cross over."

"But what were you doing in Holms' barn?" Peter asked. "For it was you, of course."

"If one is lonesome, even cows can be companions." Uncle Victor turned away.

Peter spoke again. He was sorry for the captive, believed his story. But with so much at stake they couldn't afford to take chances.

"But it was you who were in the *konditeri* the day you posted the notices about going back to school. Why is it you can have so much liberty and the others have to go back to the barracks?"

"They don't have to go. It's by choice. When they found the Norwegians were ignoring them they decided they would stay together entirely. And then when the epidemic came they were frightened."

"Weren't you frightened, too?"

"Not I, because death, it is nothing. I live only that someday I can help my country. Poland is my country."

Uncle Victor cleared his throat. If he was going to say something, the Polish boy didn't give him a chance.

"But won't you take me with you to America, for surely that is where you are going?" He looked about the cabin. "From the other side of the fiord, I saw the boat in its clever disguise and I knew you'd be sailing soon for that country. I'll be no trouble if you take me. And when I get there I've a place to go. I have a married sister in Pittsburgh."

"But that's utter nonsense," Uncle Victor protested. And his voice was again loud and angry. "Even if I didn't think this some sly Nazi trick, how could I land you there? They wouldn't let you in without a passport."

CHAPTER TWENTY-FOUR

U NCLE VICTOR wanted to know how his prisoner came to be wearing a German army uniform and this is the story the Polish boy told:

"My name is Jan Lasek. My home is in Cracow, near the German border. I was born the year of the Armistice, 1918, when Poland declared her independence.

"Until last summer I was a student of languages at the University of Cracow. Always I wanted to go to America where I could practice my English and study it further. But there were six in our family and to spare the money was out of the question. My sister went to Pittsburgh to marry one of our countrymen. My grandmother was already living there. When grandmother died she left me some money. The legacy was in a bank in Pittsburgh and it was easier if I'd go there to get it. So I was to have a year of study in America, after all.

"All last summer when there were signs of trouble my father would say, 'Jan, you go to America.' But I had a job tutoring, and was making money, and so I waited until just before the University of Pittsburgh would open. I waited too long.

"The last week in August I went to Gdynia to take the boat for America. I had my ticket and my passport. But when I turned them in to go aboard a strange thing happened. Two men wearing police uniforms came up and took me by the shoulders.

" 'You're to come with us,' they said.

"I had to go along. There was nothing else to do. But instead of taking me where someone would tell me what was wanted of me, they threw me into a dark basement and there I stayed for two days and nights without so much as a crust of bread or a drop of water. It was because they'd forgotten me.

"In the meantime the Germans crossed into Poland and bombed, I think, twenty-three cities. But this I learned later. Then I knew only what I could guess from what had troubled my father, and from the sound of the bombs dropping all around.

"After two days they remembered about me and brought me food and water. I inquired what had happened and they told me that Germany and Poland were at war. I asked about my ticket and passport and they only shrugged.

" 'The boat left on schedule,' they said, 'Jan Lasek was aboard.'

"Little by little I began to understand. They had wanted my passport for someone else. So I was locked up, and that other is masquerading in the United States doing I don't know what harm. The men who arrested me were not Polish but German secret police in uniforms they brought with them from their own country. For in the house where I was kept prisoner, I saw every kind of uniform or costume you could think of.

"There were disguises for clergymen, even the robes for a bishop. Men's formal dress included the ribbons and medals of a diplomat. For the women were all kinds of clothing from the cap and apron of a parlour maid to the furs and jewels of a countess.

"One of the people in that house wore the black dress and inverted collar of a cleric. Here is one who will help me, I thought, before I knew about the disguises. This man of God will advise me in my troubles. One day when I had a chance, I spoke to him. 'I'm being kept here against my will,' I said. 'Will you help me to get back to my own people?'

"He laughed to put me to shame. 'So you think I make a convincing looking clergyman?' he said. 'But you flatter me.' When next I saw him he was wearing the uniform of a German Gestapo.

"But he did not hold my question against me. I thought he seemed to like me for he spoke to me often which was more than the rest of them did. One time I saw him packing a valise preparatory to going away. But first he had to unpack it. He took out the uniform of a streetcar conductor.

" 'This is what I wore when I first came to Poland two years ago.' He held up the cap for me to read the letters of its insignia and then he showed me the coat and trousers. From one of the pockets he drew out a book of streetcar tickets.

" 'I learned more about Poland in one year of riding the Warsaw tramcars than most people will know in a lifetime. And I found my knowledge very useful.'

"I asked him why so many different kinds of dress were found in one house.

" 'But it's wise to have many changes of dress. Come, I'll show you.' He opened a large wardrobe and from it he drew out a suit of Scotch tweed. Plaid cap, rough shoes and a heavy blackthorn stick went with it. Then he began practicing his Scottish dialect.

" 'The dress of a Scotsman was verra, verra helpful to me,' he mocked. 'It got me into the British Embassy and there I drew more than one piece of information out of the servants—information that was gratefully received at home.'

" 'Who wears the nurses' uniforms?' I asked.

" 'Who would wear them but our women agents? They get employment in an influential family where they can learn much that our country wishes to know. So, what does it matter if the employer or the maid furnishes the uniform? It's only a few marks one way or the other. One of our girls was able to bring us information about a depot of ammunition our other agents didn't know existed. It's been blown up!' he finished.

" 'Spies!' I said, entirely without regard of what he would do to me. But it didn't make him angry. He only shrugged his shoulders.

" 'Call us that, if you like. We describe ourselves as patriots.'

" 'Patriots? Yes, you can call yourselves that if you mean coming into a peaceful country and getting control of it by lies, sneakiness, bribery and corruption.'

" 'But that's the highest form of patriotic duty to one's own country,' he said, and I'll say this much for him. He was speaking the truth as he knew it.

"One of these disguises was given me. It was the uniform of a German army private. I had to put it on or I'd be shot.

" 'But what do you want of me?' I asked the woman who kept that house.

" 'Our Fuehrer needs your passport for work of his own in America,' she said.

" 'But why must I wear a German uniform?' I asked.

" 'You ought to be glad to wear it. You might have been left to die in the basement.'

" 'Why do I owe my life to this uniform?'

" 'You were locked in. Nobody meant you should die of starvation but you were forgotten about. We've more important things to think about than one Pole. But we needed someone who knew languages—not one or two but many foreign tongues. Your papers say you are a student of languages. So you will be an interpreter for the army.'

" 'Never,' I said. 'My country's at war with Germany and I'll do nothing to help an enemy.'

" 'Don't worry,' she said. 'In a short time there'll be no war. Poland will have surrendered.'

"One day I was taken out of that house and with a body of German guardsmen I was put on a train and sent south to my own city of Cracow.

"I was in Cracow for months after that. You can imagine my shame when one of the few old neighbors that were left saw me in a Nazi uniform.

"My father was dead. He was shot when he went to the assistance of an old priest who was dragged off the altar at mass. My mother was not there. They said she got to Rumania and took my little brother and sister. Two of my brothers died defending our city. My home

I saw. There are hardly two bricks standing on top of each other.

"I make no mention of the humiliation of our people or of how the Germans stole our money, our homes, our farms and the very potatoes in our fields. I say nothing of what they did to our priests. Or of how they took our young men and made them work at hard labor for themselves. Nor of how they turned the women and children out of their houses overnight and sold those houses to people in Germany. All these things I saw with my own eyes.

"Me they treated with civility. Always I've had enough to eat and a bed. I translate orders from the officers into whatever language is needed for posting to the civilian population—Polish there, Norwegian here. If I refused, they'd shoot me and all the while I'm hoping to live for Poland.

"Norway has seen little. It's Poland that has suffered. Here you think the Germans are decent; and they have behaved better in your country than in mine. Perhaps it is because they think of Norway as a part of Germany. So they have not yet taken all your food and left you to starve. Poland they used as an example. It was to show what would happen to you if you did not submit.

"Now you know why I am not spying on you to tell the Germans and win a promotion. You know why I've watched your children because, if you belong to a country that has been invaded as mine has, then you are drawn in sympathy to people that have similarly suffered. You know now why I must get to America."

CHAPTER TWENTY-FIVE

"WELL, what are we going to do with him?" Uncle Victor asked when Jan Lasek had finished his story. They had put him in the hold while they discussed the problem.

"We daren't turn him loose, that's certain," Rolls replied. "We can't take the risk that he won't tell the Commandant."

"He'd never do that," Peter spoke quickly.

"His story sounds true enough," Uncle Victor decided. "I can well believe what he's told us. We know about the disguises ourselves, about men who came to Norway dressed as sports lovers but who turned out to be secret police. But I think it's dangerous to let him go. Whether he meant to or not, he could accidentally say something that would put the Germans on our trail."

"But what shall we do with him?"

"He'll have to be kept in the hold. We can't stand guard over him. I've a crew coming on tomorrow, but even so I cannot spare a man just to watch him."

Rolls was laying the table for supper. Since it was so late, Peter was to spend the night aboard the *Cleng*, and there was no place on earth he would rather be. His mother would not miss him that night for he was supposed to be at the Holms' farm.

"Couldn't you take him with you to America, Uncle Victor?" Peter pleaded. "It seems a shame he can't go."

"But I *can't* take him without a passport. That's all there is to that," his uncle said shortly.

"It would be a terrible thing to go that distance and be turned back at the end," Rolls explained.

"I could sign him on as a sailor," Uncle Victor answered. "But he'd be interned because I'm not planning to return. I'm afraid that would be pretty hard on him after all he's gone through."

"You could land him somewhere along the coast where the fighting is going on," Rolls suggested. "There are Poles with the British army."

"Too dangerous," his captain replied. "Once I get out of this fiord, I'm going to stay out to sea. Overnight the Germans have been capturing our towns. I might run into an enemy occupation. Once I get past, I'm going to stay past."

The Polish boy had been frightened when they told him they would have to lock him up for the night.

"Nothing will harm you," Uncle Victor said. "You won't have to go back to the barracks. We're hiding and you can hide with us."

They had to wait for the long twilight to fade to bring in the gold that the children had buried that day. They didn't dare carry a light.

"You see now why I had you build the snowmen?" Uncle Victor asked Peter. "We just have to feel our way. So all we do is to feel for a snowman, and under him is the gold."

With three of them at work it wasn't long before they had the bullion aboard the *Cleng*.

"Fifty-one bricks," Rolls grunted in satisfaction.

"And each brick is worth five thousand United States dollars," Uncle Victor spoke cheerfully. "That's two hundred and fifty-five thousand dollars we collected from these snowmen. And quite a lot of money."

"Uncle Victor, that's just about all the gold in the cave. One day more'll bring it all out. This morning I asked Per Garson how much was left and he said a hundred bricks. Well, here are fifty-one of them right here."

"That's what I've been hoping. As soon as this Polish boy is missed, the Germans will start searching for him. They may come here. Even with the camouflage, it's dangerous if they get too close. If I had my crew, I think I would sail tonight. Although I'd have to leave the rest of the gold, I'd do it to be safe."

Before he turned in that night Rolls quizzed Jan Lasek about when he would be missed at the camp.

Jan said he *might* be missed that night, but they couldn't help noting his absence at roll call in the morning.

When Rolls told his chief, Peter thought his uncle looked solemn.

"Then the search may start tonight." He went to the porthole to look through a slit in the fir branches.

"You don't expect them here already?" Peter asked.

"No, I want to see if there's any sign of my sailors. They'll come at night."

"But the curfew, Uncle Victor?"

"It'd be a lot safer for them at night. But don't worry. Hans Torp and Sten and Dino are resourceful fellows. They'll manage. I told them to be here no later than tomorrow, and they'll be here."

There were voices out of the night beyond the portholes. From the direction of the beach came calls. Crowded at the peepholes in the fir branches, the three in the cabin waited. The voices grew louder. Outside in the snow were several squads of Germans.

"So the search has started," Victor spoke softly. "And they're even looking here. Whew! What a narrow squeak! If they'd come an hour earlier, they would have found us out there with the gold!"

CHAPTER TWENTY-SIX

I T HAD taken the Germans until taps to miss the Polish recruit.

Then the hunt for him had started.

Nearer and nearer to the *Cleng Peerson* came the searching party. But Uncle Victor was calm.

"If you couldn't find the boat in the daytime, knowing it was here, they're not going to find it at night," he comforted Peter. "So let's not worry about their finding us. I'm only hoping that Torp and the other two don't pick this time to come aboard."

The Germans trailed up the valley well beyond the two fallen trees. But here the snow was clear of footprints, as the three in the cabin knew. So their trip only served to churn the snow and widen the hunt. For with many footprints on the ground, later search parties would have more territory to cover.

Uncle Victor, Rolls and Peter continued to crowd at the peepholes in the fir branches over the ports. After a time they saw the Germans turn back towards the cliff and the beach.

"If they search the woods, they can't help coming on the ski trail of our friend here." Uncle Victor meant Jan Lasek. "That'll lead them here by the back way and you can be sure they'll do some close searching."

The next morning the Snake was quiet as always. The Germans evidently had not yet found the ski trail, and Uncle Victor hoped to be at sea before they did.

Just before dawn, Hans Torp and the two other sailors came aboard. They took turns watching for the enemy's approach, but the morning wore away and they neither saw nor heard anything. The last of the gold would be brought down that afternoon. When it was dark the *Cleng* could sail.

It was going to rain, Peter noted with satisfaction. It wouldn't matter now. The gold had been saved.

Lovisa's and Michael's teams came to the Snake that day. Peter went out to join them, for he would be going back to town with them. He longed to remain in the Snake to see Uncle Victor set sail. But for the safety of them all and for the accomplishment of all they had set out to do, he made no protest when Uncle Victor said he must go back to town.

"Oh, Peter! We did it! We did it!" Lovisa threw her arms around him. "Every last brick's out of the cave. It's all down here. We fooled them! We fooled those old goose-steppers!"

"What about the soldier that's missing?" Peter wanted to know at once. "Was there a search for him in town last night?"

"Was there? Well, you should have been at home! In the middle of the night they pounded on the door. Per Garson went to open it. They almost knocked him down pushing past him. They started searching the house. They looked in closets, even with Mother's dresses. They woke up Bunny and he started hollering. Mother told them she didn't know what they were looking for but if they'd tell her she'd know how to help them. But they just went on poking behind curtains.

Do they think we'd hide one of their men? Why are they making this fuss?"

"I guess on account of his being a Pole. And forced against his will to join their army."

"Was he? How do you know that? How do you know he's a Pole? Nobody in town said he was a Pole."

But Peter wouldn't tell. Lovisa went on:

"There's a notice on the school door. It said that anyone with information about this missing soldier must report at once to the Commandant, and if anyone is found to know something and *hasn't* told, he'll be punished with death. Ugh, these Germans!"

"Whew!" Peter whistled.

"Mother's afraid for the Holms," Lovisa went on. "She thinks the missing man might be hiding around their barn and she's going down this afternoon to warn them to get him out. For she said if they did find anyone there it'd be pretty hard to make the Nazis understand the Holms didn't want him. She'll be there when we get back."

Peter nodded. "Let's get these bricks down and get out of here."

Lovisa turned back to her sled and Peter, watching her, saw her stiffen in fright.

"Look, Peter," she whispered.

Into the Snake filed a company of German soldiers and an officer.

"They've come to search," Lovisa said.

"They did that last night. I guess they've come to look again."

"Peter, what'll we do? They'll see us with the gold."

"Right," he snapped into action. "The kids'll have to hurry. Get your bricks in the snow. Quick, team," he lowered his voice. "Here come the Germans."

Like squirrels burying nuts, the children burrowed in the snow. It flew in all directions.

"Not so deep," Peter directed. "Just lay the bricks down and start the snowmen. Faster. They're coming."

Mittened hands had unloaded the sleds. Now the snow was being patted into hard lumps. The children were well-practiced after so many months of winter. Soon was standing a fine army of snowmen.

Michael's team was farther up the valley by the farthest of the two fallen trees. Peter gave the whistle they used at school when Mr. Anders was coming.

Michael whistled back. Then he must understand.

He'd know that someone was coming, that danger was near.

"All right, Lovisa, let them come," Peter dropped on his knees in the snow and began another figure. It was easier to do that than to stand waiting for the Germans. In all the weeks they'd been coming to the Snake, this would be the first time the Germans had come there at the same time. Lovisa thought something of this, too.

"They had to wait for the very last day," she grumbled. "They let us bring every last bit of gold out. Then they come and find it."

"Shhh," Peter cautioned. "Don't let them know you think anything is out of the ordinary in their coming here. They're only looking for the runaway soldier, you know."

It was Lieutenant Sit-Down who led the company into the Snake. They came plodding through the snow to the level space between the two trees and here the ground was dotted with children and snowmen.

"There's no one here but these youngsters," he told the sergeant. "There's no use to ask them if they saw anyone for they won't answer. I think we might as well go back."

The sergeant drew up stiffly. "Pardon, Herr Lieutenant," he said, "the Commandant comes."

CHAPTER TWENTY-SEVEN

NEAR the cliff Peter could see the bulky figure of the Commandant, the head of the German forces at Riswyk. He was picking his way up the valley.

Peter and Lovisa continued playing in the snow. Peter had begun a snowman and Lovisa was making hers a fancy hat.

They wanted to get up and start for home but they didn't dare move. They felt they would be less noticed if they stayed where they were.

The Commandant came puffing along. He seemed to have trouble lifting his feet in the deep snow. In his hand he carried a light little cane, a swagger stick.

He plodded along until he came to the children. When he got there he stopped in his tracks.

"If he'd only go on," Peter growled to himself. But he didn't dare look up to see. His hands were busy with the snow. His head was hot and his mouth dry and there was a buzzing in his ears.

What would happen now? What if the Commandant found the bricks buried under the snowmen. Why there were more than a million kroner right here at their feet!

"We're searching for a German infantryman," the Commandant announced to the children. "Have any of you seen a man in these woods?"

Of course, there was no answer. He turned aside to whisper a few words to Lieutenant Sit-Down. Then he spoke to the children in a loud voice:

"I said we are looking for a German infantryman. It's very important for you children to tell if you've seen one on this part of the coast. There's a severe penalty attached if anyone has seen him and has not reported it."

Still the children said nothing.

"I've a good mind to give you children a lesson in manners," his voice was angry. "When you're spoken to, it's only right that you should answer. Has no one taught you that? Now then. Yes or no? Have you seen a German infantry soldier in this fiord?"

The children acted as if they had not heard him. Lovisa sat back on her heels to admire her handiwork. But Peter, for all he tried to be cool, felt a terrible thumping in his chest. His cheeks must be red as rowan-berries. For if any snowman were to be knocked down—

The Commandant strode across the snow and stood above Lovisa.

"Little girl, tell me, did you or did you not see a German infantryman?" he screamed in anger. "Answer me."

Lovisa only turned her big blue eyes up at him. Not so much as a nod did she give him.

"Don't you know I can make you talk? Don't you realize that we Germans can make anyone do our will? We've only to command to be obeyed."

Peter remembered the pact they had made the day they had started their undertaking. They had sworn on the sword they wouldn't give information about what they were doing. Of course, this wasn't the same. But even so, they weren't to talk to the Germans for fear they would say something to make them suspicious. But no need to worry about Lovisa. Pledge or not, she wouldn't talk.

The Commandant's eye fell. There was something he didn't like about Lovisa's snowman.

"Bah, you Norwegians!" With his stick he slashed off the snowman's head. It was as if he would do the same to Lovisa's. Then he raised the stick and cut the snowman neatly in two. The upper part rolled beside the head. Only the haunches remained.

"Down you go," he shouted in his rage. "Just the way all people go who stand in our Fuehrer's way. The way Norway goes. And Holland and Belgium and France and England and all countries that oppose the German will."

Lovisa was near to tears, Peter could tell. But she winked them back.

"Now, little girl," the Commandant went on, "you see what will happen to all your people if you do not help the good Germans who have come to save you from the hardships your country makes you endure."

"Hardships!" Peter had to bite his tongue to keep from saying. "It's you who bring the hardships, you with your talk of 'the good Germans.'"

"So, little girl, let this be a lesson." The high officer was still in a rage. "Unless you want yourself and all who belong to you to go rolling over like that—and that—and that—"

He began kicking the stump of Lovisa's snowman. The snow flew out in a shower. With each kick, Peter winced. For the Commandant's foot could only be a few inches from her two bricks. In their haste that day they had not been able to bury deep but had to count on the snowmen to hide the gold.

The high officer had evidently decided to give Lovisa a thorough lesson for he lifted his foot for another kick. Like a football player he stood back to swing at what was left of the snow figure.

"In another minute he'll stub his toe against the bricks," Peter thought.

Then he gathered up a handful of snow. He rolled it into a hard ball. Then he stood back and took aim.

It landed exactly on the Commandant's right ear as Peter meant it should.

Then Peter took to his heels and ran for the woods.

CHAPTER TWENTY-EIGHT

"THERE he goes! After him!"

Peter had little chance to escape. Lieutenant Sit-Down and almost his whole company were chasing him.

But Peter knew these woods and the foreigners did not. He hoped to cross the Snake above where it was narrower and take the ski trail up the mountain. In the forest above he had a good chance to hide.

But he was cut off before he could get upstream far enough to cross. The Germans spread out in a circle and blocked all points. Peter felt like a rabbit facing a pack of hounds.

Rough arms were around him and he fell to the ground. There was a tussle, and Peter all but succeeded in throwing off his captor. But the others came up and he was one against many, a boy surrounded by men.

There was nothing to do but submit. They dragged him to his feet. He fell in step with them. They were marching him off to their barracks.

But the snowball trick had worked!

He had succeeded in distracting the Commandant. The outrage of being snowballed by a Norwegian boy was enough to make him forget the lesson he was giving Lovisa—showing her how the Norse would be treated by the German conquerors. And so, he had not uncovered the gold she had buried beneath the very snowman he was kicking.

Yes, the snowball trick had worked! When Peter was led back to the place between the two fallen trees, he saw the Commandant was leaving. The snowmen were still standing and the children were filing out of the Snake.

Peter did not mind being a German prisoner if he had saved the gold.

How much of this had Uncle Victor seen? he wondered. No doubt every bit of it.

But could he do anything to help him?

Frightened as he was, not knowing what was going to happen, he still didn't want any aid from Uncle Victor. His uncle's only concern was to get the gold out of Norway. If he did that, it was all that anyone could expect of him.

But Uncle Victor wasn't the one to let a fellow down, Peter knew. He had always been ready to help before.

But in a case like this, with so much—the money, maybe their very lives—involved, Peter didn't think his uncle could do much.

A soldier marched on his right and one on his left. Ahead and behind were others. When they reached the sentries, these sprang up, their rifles on their shoulders. So they were quite a little company when they turned into the barracks they had built before the fishing wharf.

The heavy boots of the Nazis clumped in rhythm over the wooden boards of the barracks floor. Thump, thump, thump, thump, down a long hallway they pounded. Then they stopped. Peter was shoved into a box of a room no bigger than a clothes closet. A key was turned in the door. Then the thump, thump, thump of the soldiers as they left him alone in the twilight.

He stumbled against something like a low shelf. It was supposed to be his bed, he guessed. There was a window at one end of the tiny room. It was barred. Through it he could see the beach, snow-covered to the very edge of the black lapping water. Through the snow the sentry stepped, up and down, up and down, his legs swinging straight out from his hips like those of a toy soldier wound with a key.

What were they going to do with him, Peter wondered. Would he be tried at a court martial?

Up past the window stepped the sentry. Then he turned and followed his own footprints back in the direction he had come.

Was it a serious offense to snowball a high German officer? Peter believed it was. It had something to do with order and respect for authority. Well, he didn't care how serious it was. They could shoot him if they liked. He was glad he had thrown that snowball.

But still, he was horribly afraid.

Would even the Germans put a boy to death? He couldn't be sure. From the stories of what they did in Poland, he could believe almost anything. Still, these Germans in Norway didn't seem so bad. The captain who had gone away had moved his troops out of their sled track, and they had all been very decent and had kept to themselves and had not even raided the food supplies as they had done in other countries. They had all been very friendly except this Commandant. But even he had offered to have an orderly help Mrs. Lundstrom pull the sled on which Bunny and the others sat on thousands of kroner of gold.

But Jan's story of Poland kept coming back—of how they had turned the people out of their houses and had taken the priest off the altar at mass.

When he thought of Jan his mouth was hot and dry again. For whether or not he was in serious trouble for having snowballed the Commandant, he knew he would be if it were known he'd seen the escaped Pole. Lovisa said there was a notice on the school door saying that anyone who was found to know something about him and not telling would be punished by death.

By death.

How cold it was in this barracks! Even in his windbreaker and heavy outdoor clothes he felt cold. His teeth were coming together and apart like hammers.

The sun had gone down and there was only a dim grey light coming from the inside. It seemed to be raining. Maybe that was why it got dark so early. Anyway, the northern afternoon was over. Outside it all seemed so wet and sad, down here by the fishing pier.

After a time a soldier came to the door. He brought Peter a deep dish of stew and some dark bread.

The soldier spoke to him. "I come back to get your dish. Then I will take you to the Commandant," he said in German.

Peter couldn't eat. He tried to but it was no use.

Later there were footsteps in the hall. A key turned in the lock. The time was up. The soldier had come to take him to the Commandant. He stepped into the cell. Even in the dim light Peter could tell it was not the same soldier.

CHAPTER TWENTY-NINE

THE SOLDIER came inside and shut the door and leaned against it.

Peter looked hard at him. He could see so little from the streak of light from the window. But there was something familiar.

The soldier was Jan Lasek, the Pole. But, no. That couldn't be. Jan was on Uncle Victor's boat in the Snake. Peter had seen him there that day.

"Shhhh," Jan put his finger to his lips. From his tunic pocket he dug a scrap of paper. It was so dark Peter had to go over and over it before he could make it out. It was a note from Uncle Victor. Peter read:

"Jan Lasek is risking his liberty and perhaps his life for you. Follow him at all costs, wherever he goes. On that depends your safety and his."

There was no signature but Peter knew well his uncle's bold handwriting. He nodded to show he understood.

Jan kept listening for a sound. What was he waiting for, Peter dared not ask. From afar Peter could make out a kind of din, a rattle like knives and forks, pans and mugs. When the rattle became much louder Jan seemed satisfied. He looked out of the door. He stepped outside and closed it.

When he came back into the cell there was high excitement in his whisper.

"Come now," he said, "quickly!"

They were out in the hall. Jan stopped to turn the key in the lock outside the door where Peter had been kept prisoner. Into his pocket went the key.

And now Peter could hear the tramp, tramp, tramp, of boots. It came from a distant end of the barracks but it grew noisier with each step.

"We'll have to run," Jan whispered.

All the time the sound of the marching soldiers came closer. They seemed to be coming down a hall that would meet the corridor at right angles. And now Peter could hear nothing because of sound in his own ears. He wanted to run in the opposite direction. Why go this way? he wondered. We'll only run into them.

The marching men must be nearing the corner. But Jan only kept going faster towards them. Uncle Victor said he was to follow Jan at all costs. So behind him ran the breathless frightened Peter.

And now, on the right, Peter saw a door. Through it Jan pulled him. There was just time to close it softly. The Germans were turning the corner as Peter could tell by the sound of their steps on the other side of the door.

Peter fell into the wet snow of the beach. They were outside the barracks and, for the moment, safe.

Jan flattened himself against the wall of the building and Peter stood up beside him. The shadow of the barracks hid them. The rain was loud on the crusted snow.

"We're lucky the sentry was going up the beach, not down," Jan whispered. "Otherwise he'd have seen the light when we opened the door."

Peter felt a throbbing in his ears. He tried not to pant

but his breath was loud. Now there was another soft pod, pod, pod—more marching. Against the snow they could see a dark figure. It was the sentry returning. He walked up to a point on a line with the door, the very door over which he stood guard. He was not ten feet away from where Jan and Peter were flattened against the wall.

Slap, slap, slap, his heavy leather mittens thumped his shoulders. He changed his rifle from one side to the other and changed it back again. Then he turned and began goose-stepping back in the direction he had come.

Jan tugged at Peter's sleeve. It was now or never, he seemed to say.

Peter was not prepared for what happened next. Jan led him down the beach to the very edge of the fiord and then right into the water itself.

The cold water bit his body. The breath left him. He didn't think he could stand another minute of it. He wanted to run back to the beach but Jan kept wading out and Peter, remembering the warning in the note, found himself following him.

It seemed forever, these few minutes they waded in the water. And now Jan was swimming and Peter found himself doing the same. But you couldn't swim in that close-to-frozen water. You had no strength. Peter felt the breath going out of him. But somehow or other it seemed better to freeze to death out here than to stay in those barracks and wait for no one knew what. Then there was a numbness over him. He closed his eyes.

He must be dreaming for nothing like this could happen in real life. A hand reached out and grabbed his arm and he was pulled into a boat. Someone put a flask to his mouth and told him to drink. But the fiery stuff made him sputter and it ran down over his chin. A heavy coat was put over him and a pair of arms were cradling him.

Rolls, Uncle Victor's mate, was holding him. There was another sodden mass on the bottom of the boat. It was Jan Lasek. Peter heard them say his name.

But now he found he was beyond caring about anything. The boat, he knew, was the *Cleng Peerson's* lifeboat. Strong arms were pulling it towards the fishing smack.

CHAPTER THIRTY

PETER was dry and warm in Uncle Victor's cabin.
The coast of Norway was somewhere out in the
blackness. The Atlantic rolled and the *Cleng Peerson* pitched and Peter was jounced up and down with
the wash of the waves.

Ahead lay America.

So Peter was going to America!

He was going to see New York and go to Pittsburgh
with Jan Lasek and then travel to Minnesota where his
uncle was a professor in St. Olaf's College in North-
field.

Uncle Victor could arrange it, he said.

"You can be admitted as a minor in my custody. Our
minister in Washington will do that much for us. He'll
be only too glad to do something in return for all this
gold."

"But what about Jan Lasek?" Peter asked. "How can
he go without a passport?"

"But he *has* a passport—the one that was stolen.
There'll be a record of it in Washington and they'll be
grateful for the information about the one who is masquerading in his name. They won't be long finding him."

Peter was overjoyed with this good news for Jan.
Since he had risked his life for him, there was no re-
ward too high. Uncle Victor said something like this.

"It wasn't as easy for Jan as it looks, Peter. He ran a
grave risk. He did it simply because I didn't feel right

about sailing and leaving you there. Of course, he knew the routine of the camp. He knew that at supper hour the barracks would be deserted, except for the mess hall. And he knew about the side door and the sentry. But he was still in danger of being caught himself. If one little thing had gone wrong, he would have been caught."

"He had his uniform, too," Peter mused. "One German uniform looks pretty much like another."

Then a thought struck him. "But how did he get the key to open the cell door?" he wanted to know.

"The keys are kept on a panel in the guard room. The room was empty while the guard was at mess. All Jan had to do was to slip in and take the key marked "das Gefängnis."

His uncle went on. "All that part was easy. The only hard part was getting him to the barracks without his being seen on the way there. For he was being looked for everywhere. So we didn't dare have him go by foot from the Snake to the beach and barracks."

"It was Rolls who solved it for us," his uncle went on. "He suggested that, since the roads were being watched, we make a landing by water. The *Cleng* was pretty well covered by camouflage so she could be moved to the mouth of the Snake where it meets the big fiord. We were lucky it was a bad night. The rain and mist shortens the day. When it got dark Rolls and Hans Torp and Sten lowered the lifeboat and rowed him right up to the fishing pier. But they couldn't wait for him because it was too dangerous. They had to get back to the cover of the *Cleng*. That's why you had to swim so far."

"But how did Jan get past the sentries into the barracks?"

"Just the way you got out. He waited for one to come up, turn and start back. The minute his back was turned, he stepped inside the door. It isn't bolted till taps and Jan knew that. The sentry was there to guard that very door but there are ways to get past sentries if you can think of those ways."

"Wasn't Jan afraid he'd be caught when he got inside the barracks?"

"Of course. Terribly. But he had to risk it."

"He did it for me?"

"For you and because I said I'd take him to America if he got you out."

"We heard the soldiers marching in the hallway. Were they coming to get me?"

"Whether they were or not, you and Jan would have been in a pretty tight place if you'd run into them."

Peter fell back in the bunk. "So I'm to go to America. But what about Mother and Lovisa and Bunny?"

"Peter, I know you think it high-handed of me to be taking you this long distance without so much as asking if you wanted to go. But there was nothing else to do with you. I couldn't go all the way across the Atlantic Ocean without knowing what would become of you. And when I got you on board there was nothing to do with you but to take you along. We daren't turn back with all this gold."

"Oh, Uncle Victor, it isn't that. Only—only—"

"Only what?"

"Well, when Father left, he said I was the man of the family and was to look after the others."

"Peter, don't worry about your mother's not being able to look out for herself and for her children. And although I'm sorry to have to tell you this, your father may soon be home. The British have withdrawn their forces from much of the coast. Our army is putting up a magnificent defense but it's only a question of time until it can no longer hold out. Then the order will come to cease firing."

Peter thought about the night his father had gone away, the night of the first blackout. And of all the things that had happened since.

"It's a shame, Peter, for you to be leaving without so much as saying good-by to your family and Helga and Michael and Per Garson and the others. But your mother was glad when I told her what we were going to try to do. You know she had gone to the Holms to warn them that the missing Nazi might be in their barn. When Lovisa got to the farm with the news of what happened to you she strapped on her skis and took the back trail through the woods to the Snake.

" 'Take him to America by all means,' she said. 'I want him to grow up in a country where people are free.' She asked to have you promise that you will always remember you come of liberty-loving people who think freedom is a greater heritage than gold."

There was a clatter of steps in the companionway. Rolls came into the cabin.

"Submarine off sta'board," he said

Uncle Victor jumped to his feet in alarm. Then he saw the sheepish grin on Rolls' face.

"But it's a British sub," he spoke lamely. "The *Cleng*'s doing five knots in this sea," he added.

"She ought to ride well," Uncle Victor answered. "She's got a cargo of gold for ballast."

The flag of Norway was draped above the map on the bulkhead.

Into the cabin came the notes of a cornet.

"It's my old horn. I lent it to the Polish boy," Rolls explained.

In the galley Jan Lasek was practicing "The Star Spangled Banner."